Our Miss Brooks

A Comedy in Three Acts

FOR FIVE MEN AND TWELVE WOMEN

CHARACTERS

MISS BROOKS.................*a high school English teacher*
MISS FINCH............................*the librarian*
HUGO LONGACRE......................*the athletic coach*
MR. WADSWORTH................*the high school principal*
MISS AUDUBON........................*the music teacher*
ELSIE
ELAINE
JANE
SYLVIA
DORIS
MARGE } ....*students*
FAITH
RHONDA
TED
STANLEY
MARTIN
MRS. ALLEN............................*Rhonda's mother*

PLACE: *Miss Brooks' classroom.*

TIME: *The present. Spring.*

SYNOPSIS

ACT ONE: *Late afternoon.*

ACT TWO: *Afternoon, several weeks later.*

ACT THREE: *The night of the school play, a week later.*

CHART OF STAGE POSITIONS

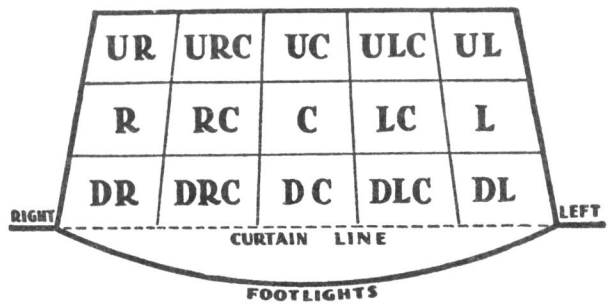

STAGE POSITIONS

Upstage means away from the footlights, *downstage* means toward the footlights, and *right* and *left* are used with reference to the actor as he faces the audience. R mean *right*, L means *left*, U means *up*, D means *down*, C means *center*, and these abbreviations are used in combination, as: U R for *up right*, R C for *right center*, D L C for *down left center*, etc. One will note that a position designated on the stage refers to a general territory, rather than to a given point.

NOTE: Before starting rehearsals, chalk off your stage or rehearsal space as indicated above in the *Chart of Stage Positions*. Then teach your actors the meanings and positions of these fundamental terms of stage movement by having them walk from one position to another until they are familiar with them. The use of these abbreviated terms in directing the play saves time, speeds up rehearsals, and reduces the amount of explanation the director has to give to his actors.

Our Miss Brooks

A COMEDY IN THREE ACTS

BY

CHRISTOPHER SERGEL

ADAPTED FROM THE ORIGINAL
MATERIAL OF

R. J. MANN

QUOTATIONS FROM ''LOST HORIZON''
BY PERMISSION OF JAMES HILTON

THE DRAMATIC PUBLISHING COMPANY

*** NOTICE ***

The amateur acting rights to this work are controlled exclusively by THE DRAMATIC PUBLISHING COMPANY without whose permission in writing no performance of it may be given. Royalty fees are given in our current catalogue and are subject to change without notice. Royalty must be paid every time a play is performed whether or not it is presented for profit and whether or not admission is charged. A play is performed anytime it is acted before an audience. All inquiries concerning amateur rights should be addressed to:

DRAMATIC PUBLISHING
P. O. Box 129., Woodstock, Illinois 60098

COPYRIGHT LAW GIVES THE AUTHOR OR THE AUTHOR'S AGENT THE EXCLUSIVE RIGHT TO MAKE COPIES. This law provides authors with a fair return for their creative efforts. Authors earn their living from the royalties they receive from book sales and from the performance of their work. Conscientious observance of copyright law is not only ethical, it encourages authors to continue their creative work. This work is fully protected by copyright. No alterations, deletions or substitutions may be made in the work without the prior written consent of the publisher. No part of this work may be reproduced or transmitted in any form or by any means, electronic or mechanical, including photocopy, recording, videotape, film, or any information storage and retrieval system, without permission in writing from the publisher. It may not be performed either by professionals or amateurs without payment of royalty. All rights, including but not limited to the professional, motion picture, radio, television, videotape, foreign language, tabloid, recitation, lecturing, publication, and reading are reserved. *On all programs this notice should appear:*

"Produced by special arrangement with
THE DRAMATIC PUBLISHING COMPANY of Woodstock, Illinois"

©MCML by
THE DRAMATIC PUBLISHING COMPANY
© Renewed MCMLXXVIII by
CHRISTOPHER SERGEL

Based upon the same material on which the well-known radio serial is based. Excerpts from "Lost Horizon" ©MCMXLII by
THE DRAMATIC PUBLISHING COMPANY

Based upon the book, "Lost Horizon ©MCMXXXIII by
WILLIAM MORROW & CO., INC.

Printed in the United States of America
All Rights Reserved
(OUR MISS BROOKS)

ISBN 0-87129-253-X

NOTES ON CHARACTERS AND COSTUMES

MISS BROOKS: She is in her late twenties, attractive, poised, very human, and consequently very well liked and respected by the students. Her humor at times is on the caustic side, but it is never meant to hurt intentionally. In Act One, she wears a spring dress or suit; in Act Two, she has on work clothes—perhaps some old slacks and a man's shirt. If this is not practical, any other clothes that are obviously work clothes will do. She wears a semi-formal dress in Act Three.

MISS FINCH: She is about the same age as Miss Brooks, pretty, likable, and matter of fact. In Acts One and Two, she wears spring dresses. She may wear something dressier for Act Three.

HUGO: Hugo is in his twenties; he is well built, with natural good looks. He takes his position as athletic coach a little too seriously, but he is sincere and hard working. He wears slacks and a T shirt in Act One. In Act Two, he wears slacks and a sports jacket. He wears a suit in Act Three.

MR. WADSWORTH: He is in his forties, a big man with a perpetually harassed air. He is aware of his importance as school principal, and never lets you forget it. Throughout the play his suits are immaculately pressed, his ties tied to perfection.

MISS AUDUBON: She is in her late thirties, high-strung and fluttery, exhibiting a well developed case of teacher's nerves. In Acts One and Two, she dresses conservatively and practically. In Act Three, she wears a frilly, girlish semi-formal dress and a large corsage. She has even acquired a new hair-do for the occasion.

JANE: She is a sweet girl of seventeen, quiet and unassuming, but with much natural charm. She wears school clothes in Act One. In Act Two, she is dressed in old dungarees and an older sweater. Her hair is done up, to avoid being splattered with paint. In Act Three, she is dressed and made up for the part she is to play in "Lost Horizon." This costume consists of a simple but attractive dress for an older girl. Her hair is suitably arranged.

TED: He is a husky boy of eighteen, well-liked, and not the least bit conceited. He wears sports clothes in Acts One and Two. In Act Three, he is dressed for the part of Conway. He wears a tweed suit, and his hair is slicked back. If desired, he may wear a neat mustache.

RHONDA: She is seventeen, an attractive girl, but vain and selfish. She is not liked by the students, but this fact doesn't bother Rhonda. She wears school clothes in Act One. In Act Two, she wears an attractive Chinese kimono. She wears the same kimono in Act Three, but she is made up as a Chinese girl.

MRS. ALLEN: Mrs. Allen is in her forties, a pushing, domineering woman, with a highly affected manner. She wears a spring suit in Act Two. In Act Three, she is over-dressed in a semi-formal gown.

OTHER STUDENTS: They are a group of high school students, of various types and personalities. They wear school clothes. In Act Three, all but Sylvia and Martin are in costume for the parts they are to play in "Lost Horizon." Sylvia, who is the stage manager, wears a simple dress. Martin, who plays the High Lama, has not put on his costume when the act begins. Elaine, Faith, and Marge wear evening dresses, with their hair done up. Doris is dressed and made up as a pretty Chinese serving-girl. Elsie may be dressed to portray the part of the prickly little missionary lady in a tweed suit, with hat and walking stick. Stanley may portray a handsome young Englishman.

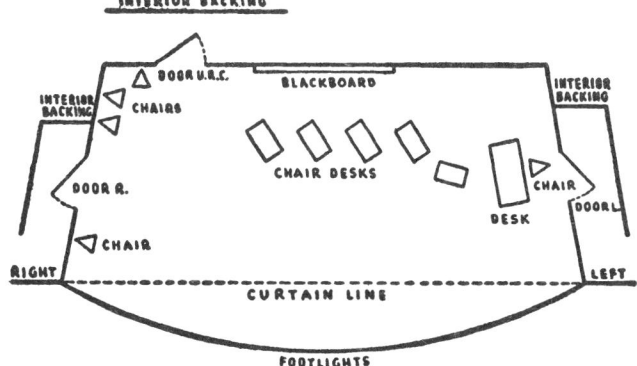

PROPERTIES

GENERAL: Blackboard, chalk and erasers, Miss Brooks' desk and chair, accessories for desk, row of school chair-desks, several other chairs, wastebasket, properties for "Lost Horizon": (Act Two), spotlight on stand (Act Two), slat of wood (Act Two), large mirror on Miss Brooks' desk (Act Three), make-up articles on Miss Brooks' desk (Act Three), small mirror on one of the student's desks (Act Three).

MISS BROOKS: Travel folders, Jane's papers in desk drawer, other papers in desk drawer, single sheet of paper, box of Kleenex, watch.

TED: Armload of basketballs, pipe.

FAITH: Handkerchief, playbook.

MR. WADSWORTH: Playbook.

ELAINE: Handkerchief, playbook.

RHONDA: Handkerchief.

JANE: Stack of playbooks, pail of paint and brushes, armload of band instruments, vase (belonging to Mrs. Allen).

SYLVIA: Clip board, paper, pencil, watch.

MISS AUDUBON: Papers.

MARTIN: Slip of paper, papers (lines from play).

DORIS: Boxes of soap flakes, bill for soap flakes, large piece of tin.
MARGE: Large cardboard box containing drapes.
MISS FINCH: Two books.
STANLEY: Bicycle.
MRS. ALLEN: Two Chinese vases.
ELSIE: Playbook, paper and pencil.
BASKETBALL PLAYER: Basketball.
COACH: Robe and playbook.

ACT ONE

SCENE: *A typical high school classroom. There is a blackboard against the wall* U C. *A large desk and chair are* L. *In front of it is a row of students' chair-desks. Another chair-desk is* L C. *Several other chairs are about the room at* R *stage. There are doors* L, R, *and* U R C.]

AT RISE OF CURTAIN: *It is late afternoon of a spring day.* MISS BROOKS *is sitting at the desk* L, *glancing at some travel folders.* TED, *a husky student, is standing with his back to the audience, facing the blackboard. After a moment of meditation he sighs, takes a piece of chalk, and writes, "I should not copy other people's examination papers." He regards his work for a moment, and then turns towards* MISS BROOKS.]

TED [*quietly*]. Miss Brooks. [*With a slight edge in his voice.*] Miss Brooks. [MISS BROOKS *puts down folders and looks at him.* TED, *having caught her attention, clears his throat and speaks in his most winning tone.*] You're kidding—aren't you? [*He nods invitingly.* MISS BROOKS *shakes her head.* TED *considers her thoughtfully a moment. Then he speaks; it is a simple statement of fact.*] You're *not* kidding. [MISS BROOKS *shakes her head slowly and firmly, then goes back to her reading.* TED *ponders this awful fact for a moment.*] Has it ever struck you that I'm a pretty adult sort of person? [*Without looking up,* MISS BROOKS *gives a brief shake of her head.* TED *makes a last desperate try, his voice pitched higher.*] Do you honestly think it's going to help my education to write a hundred times on the blackboard, "I should not copy other people's examination papers"?

MISS BROOKS. I honestly don't know.

TED [*pressing what he thinks is an advantage*]. You're a modern teacher—an up-to-date teacher—why would *you* insist on a medieval thing like this?

MISS BROOKS [*wondering, herself, looking out front*]. Queer, isn't it? [TED *nods emphatically.*] I just had an overpowering whim. Every year at this time, I get overpowering whims.

TED [*meaning to be helpful*]. Maybe it's a vitamin deficiency. The coach was telling me——

MISS BROOKS [*turning to him*]. The coach will be worrying about you. Better start writing.

TED. Miss Brooks—I'm not the ungallant type—you know me—but Rhonda Allen wasn't exactly hiding her paper. In fact——

MISS BROOKS [*agreeing*]. She probably had a whim.

TED [*nodding, defeated*]. Probably.

MISS BROOKS. Start writing.

TED [*regarding his first line*]. Couldn't we tighten up this sentence a little? Make it a little more punchy? More direct to the point? How about just—"I shouldn't copy"?

MISS BROOKS. That tightens it up.

TED [*pressing harder*]. How about plain, simple, direct—"I shouldn't"?

MISS BROOKS. But that doesn't give the whole meaning. Shouldn't what?

TED. You know—whatever I do—[*Writes on blackboard as he speaks.*]—"I shouldn't." [MISS BROOKS *shakes her head at him.* TED *sighs and adds "copy" after it.* MISS BROOKS *smiles at him as he industriously and laboriously starts writing line over and over again.*]

[MISS FINCH *enters* L *and crosses to the upstage side of* MISS BROOKS' *desk.*]

MISS FINCH. I thought you'd be hiding out.

MISS BROOKS [*with a smile*]. You think I'd better?

MISS FINCH. You've got the boss muttering again. Even in the library! I put a senior in charge and got out. [*Notices* TED.] What's he doing?

TED [*over his shoulder*]. It's a whim. [*Continues writing.*]

MISS FINCH [*crossing to* TED, *speaking back to* MISS BROOKS *as she goes*]. Are you crazy? [*Turns* TED'S *face around so she can recognize it, and then turns it back.*] That's Ted Wilder. [*Without turning around,* TED *nods vigorously.*] He should be in the gym practicing. [TED *nods again.* MISS FINCH *turns to* MISS BROOKS.] Do you have a big bet on against our basketball team?

MISS BROOKS [*with mock surprise*]. You mean Ted Wilder needs to practice? [TED *shakes his head with mock horror at such a thought.*]

MISS FINCH [*coming in front of* MISS BROOKS]. I mean the coach will probably brain you with a discus or a sixteen-pound shot.

MISS BROOKS [*smiling*]. If he does, I'll complain to the principal.

MISS FINCH. The last time I heard the principal, he didn't sound as though he'd care.

MISS BROOKS. When was that?

MISS FINCH. About three minutes ago. Has it ever occurred to you that when the daughter of the school board president enters a "Best Theme" contest, it calls for a little special consideration?

MISS BROOKS. I considered Rhonda Allen's theme. I even considered Rhonda Allen.

MISS FINCH. Then gave the prize to Jane Drew.

MISS BROOKS [*shrugging*]. Jane wrote the best theme.

MISS FINCH. You said you considered Rhonda Allen.

MISS BROOKS [*nodding*]. When that girl gets out of school she'll meet hundreds of people who won't be the least impressed by her mother being president of the school board. [*Innocently.*] I'm trying to prepare Rhonda for the future.

TED [*turning around*]. Do you mind if I say something?

MISS BROOKS. Yes. [TED *nods in a resigned way, and turns back to his work.*]

MISS FINCH [*to* MISS BROOKS]. You'd better be thinking about your own future.

MISS BROOKS. I am! I'm thinking about my near future. Did you ever dream about a vacation, that's a *vacation?* [*Holds up several travel folders.*] All expense cruise to San Juan, Jamaica, Caracas—or eleven days to Haiti and Cuba—two hundred thirty-five dollars.

MISS FINCH [*drily*]. And up. I took a cruise once. Seven school teachers to every male. [*Sits on end of a student's desk.*]

MISS BROOKS [*happily oblivious*]. Just for example, take the fourth day: [*Reads from folder.*] "In the morning, an English-speaking driver-guide in a private car will conduct you on a sightseeing tour. You'll drive to a mointaintop resort seven thousand feet above sea level, and stop there for lunch. The scenery is beyond description! [*Swallows.*] You can see coffee, cacao, bananas, coconuts, sugar——"

MISS FINCH [*cutting in*]. You can see that at a delicatessen.

MISS BROOKS [*proceeding firmly*]. "——mahogany, and other tropical flora." [*Eagerly.*] Would you like to hear about the fifth day?

MISS FINCH. I think the principal might drop in any minute. Wouldn't it look better if you were correcting papers?

[ELSIE, *a student, sticks her head in at the door* R.]

ELSIE. Miss Brooks—are you casting the senior play in here?

MISS BROOKS [*shaking her head*]. No, dear. See Miss Audubon next door.

ELSIE. I thought it was here. [*Goes out* R.]

MISS BROOKS. I've till the end of June to raise two hundred and thirty-five dollars—and up.

MISS FINCH. Where would a school teacher get two hundred and thirty-five dollars? [MISS BROOKS *shrugs.*] Is that all you want out of life?

MISS BROOKS [*nodding*]. A vacation—and a husband. And I'd like them simultaneously.

MISS FINCH [*shaking her head*]. Seven school teachers to every male. The odds are terrible. [*Rises.*] Now, if you'd consider going to Alaska——

MISS BROOKS [*back at her folder*]. "The scenery is beyond description!"

MISS FINCH. At least will you send Ted to basketball practice? Why do you do things like this? Is it because of your feud with the coach? Are you mad at him again?

MISS BROOKS [*shaking her head*]. It's more because I'm fond of Ted.

TED [*delighted, putting down chalk and turning around*]. And I'm very fond of you——

MISS BROOKS [*firmly*]. Keep working.

TED [*deflated, turning back to blackboard*]. Yes, Miss Brooks. [*Continues to write.*]

MISS BROOKS [*happy at the thought*]. I'm not putting on the play this year, and that means I don't have to feud with the coach. [*Recalls with shudder.*] Those battles over the use of the gym, and a few of his precious athletes——

MISS FINCH [*moving upstage of* MISS BROOKS' *desk*]. The way you and the coach went at it—I began to think maybe there was something between you.

MISS BROOKS [*shocked*]. Between us?

MISS FINCH [*firmly*]. That's right. There was some talk, you know.

MISS BROOKS. The trouble is—there's no truth in it.

MISS FINCH. Too bad.

MISS BROOKS [*nodding dolefully*]. Isn't it?

MISS FINCH [*smiling*]. Anyway—the music teacher always wanted the play, and now she's got it.

MISS BROOKS [*fervently, but sincerely*]. And I wish her well.

[ELAINE, *another student, enters* R.]

ELAINE. Are you casting the play now, Miss Brooks?

MISS BROOKS [*gesturing*]. See Miss Audubon.

ELAINE [*shrugging*]. I heard you were doing it again. [MISS BROOKS *shakes her head, and* ELAINE *goes out* R.]

MISS FINCH. I'd rather have Miss Audubon direct the play than band practice. You can hear the trombones all the way up to the library.

MISS BROOKS. You should hear them from where you're standing. [*Points* L.] That partition between me and the music room vibrates like a harp string.

MISS FINCH. This is a very convenient location. On the other side you have the gymnasium.

MISS BROOKS [*nodding*]. From that side I hear healthy young voices, raised to a shrill squeal.

MISS FINCH. That reminds me—[*Moves* R.]—I'd better get back to the library—even though it's deserted. [*A bright idea.*] Now, if I could get the school board to okay a television set——

MISS BROOKS. Thanks for warning me——[*Gestures upward with her eyes.*]—about the boss's muttering.

MISS FINCH [*seriously*]. Don't think for a minute he wanted you to make an unfair award of that prize. He's just hating life because Rhonda Allen didn't write the best theme.

MISS BROOKS. I suppose even principals have problems.

MISS FINCH [*emphatically*]. Principals have problems. School boards have problems. Teachers have problems. It's only the students that don't have any problems.

TED [*turning, indignantly*]. Is that so!

MISS FINCH [*decidedly*]. Yes, that's so. [*Goes out* R.]

TED [*looking after her for a moment*]. She's very cynical—for a librarian. [MISS BROOKS *looks up and starts to count his lines on blackboard.* TED *watches her a moment.*] You're getting pretty cynical for an English teacher. [MISS BROOKS *finishes counting and looks at* TED *with her eyebrows raised.* TED *speaks in exasperation.*] Yes, Miss Brooks. [*Returns to his work.*]

[JANE *enters* R.]

JANE [*nodding back toward* R]. They're having a lot of trouble casting the play. [*Crosses to* L C.]

MISS BROOKS [*making herself even more comfortable in her chair, contentedly*]. Don't even tell me about it.

TED [*putting down chalk*]. I ought to try out for the play.

JANE [*turning to him*]. You! [*With suppressed feeling.*] You —*copier!*

MISS BROOKS. Never mind, Jane. [*Nods towards blackboard.*] He's paying his debt to society.

TED. I'd be good in the play. I get bored winning basketball games. There's not much point in just going on and on and on winning basketball games.

MISS BROOKS [*with mock agreement*]. It must get tiresome. Why don't you vary your activities—try a little studying?—[*Holds up restraining hands.*]—In moderation, of course.

TED [*shaking head*]. It might interfere with my hobby.

JANE [*trying to hold back her bitterness*]. He's always over at Rhonda Allen's fussing with her father's sports car.

TED. A Jag is hard to tune. [*Does take.*] How'd you know that?

JANE [*uneasily*]. I just happen to know. [*With a touch of severity.*] If you keep test-driving that way, you'll have an accident. [*Sits at one of desks.*]

MISS BROOKS. Why not try a nice, quiet desk? You're worth saving, Ted. Your mind isn't altogether a blank.

JANE [*too quick, too decided*]. Oh, no! It isn't! [*They both turn and look at her.*] I mean—why would *his* mind be a blank—[*Swallows.*]—necessarily?

MISS BROOKS [*to* JANE]. Why aren't *you* trying out for the play?

JANE. There isn't time—I mean, with studying, and working, and—things.

TED [*derisively*]. Isn't time! [*Accusing, as he comes toward her.*] I've seen you sitting around in the grandstand during basketball practice—sure, I have. And before—during football practice. I suppose you'll be sitting around through the baseball season, too.

JANE [*unhappily*]. I sit around a lot.

TED [*mollified*]. Anyway—you picked my three best sports. That's quite a coincidence.

MISS BROOKS. It's certainly a coincidence. Now, would you mind getting on with your work? [TED *nods, and returns to blackboard. He starts making each sentence as different as possible, as far as penmanship is concerned, from the one above it. This goes on while* MISS BROOKS *and* JANE *discuss her writing.*]

JANE [*to* MISS BROOKS]. You didn't get a chance to look over the second draft I made? [*Notices folders.*] I guess you've been pretty busy.

MISS BROOKS [*taking out some papers, smiling*]. I've marked it all up. You've made it a lot better, but I'd like to see you break up some of those long sentences. Try for a little more variety in your sentence structure.

JANE [*crossing upstage of* MISS BROOKS' *desk*]. Too much over and over again?

MISS BROOKS [*nodding, with repressed smile*]. Why don't you miss basketball practice today? See what you can do with the typewriter in my office. [*Hands her some papers.*]

TED [*without turning around*]. Might as well miss practice. Without me in it there won't be much to see.

JANE [*agreeing completely*]. No—there won't.

TED [*turning around, startled*]. Huh? [JANE, *confused, hurries out* U R C. *From time to time we hear the sound of a typewriter off* U R C. TED *looks after* JANE *for a moment. Then he turns to* MISS BROOKS.] Does she strike you as being a little peculiar?

MISS BROOKS [*nodding*]. She wants to be an English teacher someday.

TED [*looking after* JANE]. Boy! she *is* peculiar! [MISS BROOKS *darts a quick glance at* TED, *and he suddenly starts to write furiously.*]

[COACH HUGO LONGACRE *enters* R.]

COACH [*letting out a great sigh of relief at sight of* TED]. There you are!

TED [*nodding*]. Right here, Coach.

COACH [*impatiently, crossing up to him*]. You're late for practice. [*Puzzled.*] What are you doing?

TED. Miss Brooks is trying to keep my mind from being a blank.

COACH [*not understanding*]. Your mind a blank?

TED. Not any more. [*With mock appreciation.*] No, sir. I'm gradually becoming aware that I should not copy other people's examination papers.

MISS BROOKS [*pleasantly*]. There's nothing like an education.

TED. It's really wonderful.

COACH [*to* TED]. Cut out this nonsense and get on to the locker room. [*Starts* R.]

MISS BROOKS [*firmly*]. Not till he's finished.

COACH [*pausing*]. Don't be silly.

MISS BROOKS. I'm sorry, Hugo, but this is a matter of discipline.

COACH [*half pleading*]. Miss Brooks—an athletic coach named Hugo has enough problems. . . . [*As she is unmoved.*] Miss Brooks—you're not going to keep Ted Wilder from basketball!

MISS BROOKS. It bores him—he told me himself.

COACH [*turning towards* TED]. Bores him?

MISS BROOKS. He can't see much point in just going on and on and on winning basketball games. [COACH *is open-mouthed at this. The thunderstruck* TED *gives a short, somewhat silly laugh, swallows hard, turns back to blackboard, and starts writing as fast as he can.*]

COACH [*grimly*]. Will he be much longer?

MISS BROOKS. Not much.

COACH [*sitting on upper right end of* MISS BROOKS' *desk*]. I'll wait. I've a few ideas on discipline myself.

TED [*without turning*]. Coach?

COACH. Yes?

TED. Won't they be missing you in the gym?

COACH. If they can do without you, they can certainly do without me.

MISS BROOKS [*covering for* TED]. I put it a little too strong. Ted and I were joking. He didn't say anything seriously.

COACH [*relaxing*]. He better not have. [TED *shoots a grateful glance and sigh of relief at* MISS BROOKS.] Get on with it. [*Picks up several of* MISS BROOKS' *travel folders.*] Aren't these travel folders awful?

MISS BROOKS. Awful?

COACH. I suppose you're using them as examples of over-writing.

MISS BROOKS [*more concerned*]. Over-writing?

COACH. You know what those banana ports are really like.

MISS BROOKS [*shaking head*]. No. Do you?

COACH. What do you think I do all summer?

MISS BROOKS. I thought—summer camp—or something.

COACH. Not me. I want a real *vacation*.

MISS BROOKS [*beginning to see him in a new light*]. You do?

COACH [*nodding, indicating folder*]. Take this—a person could waste two hundred and thirty-five dollars.

MISS BROOKS. You mean—it's a waste?

COACH. Do you know what you'd find on a little cruise like that? [MISS BROOKS *shakes her head. He speaks with horror.*] School teachers—mobs of them!

MISS BROOKS [*her dream about shattered, though still hoping*] Did *you* ever take a trip like that?

COACH. Not *me!* I've got a little sailboat laid up in Florida—plenty of canned food and everything you need on board—I just sail to the ports I want—miss the over-crowded, over-priced cruise towns—and it's cheaper than staying home.

MISS BROOKS. Most people don't have sailboats. [*It seems unfair.*] What are most people supposed to do?

COACH [*shrugging, then back to his obsession*]. First, I'm going down by the Dry Tortugas. [MISS BROOKS *repeats the names of the places he mentions with her lips, but not speaking out loud.*] Then across to Martinique, and maybe down through the Grenadines. I think I can get back up through the Windward Passage. [*Sighs with pleasure.*]

MISS BROOKS [*her thoughts on the Gulf Stream*]. It sounds like heaven.

COACH. It makes a vacation.

MISS BROOKS [*softly*]. Martinique—the Grenadines!
COACH [*smiling*]. You're the last person I'd expect to be interested.
MISS BROOKS [*disappointed*]. I am?
COACH [*noticing TED, who is obviously interested in the conversation*]. Come on, Ted. Hurry it up.
TED. I'm having a hard time concentrating on the blackboard and at the same time keeping up with your conversation.
MISS BROOKS. Try not to overtax your brain.
TED. I'll try. [*Continues to write.*]
COACH [*to* MISS BROOKS]. For some reason, I had a very different impression of you.
TED [*without turning*]. This time of year she gets overpowering whims.
MISS BROOKS [*sharply*]. Just keep working.
COACH [*smiling*]. Those were some fights we had last year.
MISS BROOKS [*joining his smile*]. Couldn't help it, though—we had to have a school play——
COACH [*firmly*]. An athletic program——[*They both catch themselves, and relax again.*]
MISS BROOKS. These trips . . . [*An innocent question.*] You go all by yourself—entirely?
COACH [*definitely*]. The only way.
MISS BROOKS [*thoughtfully*]. It's too bad you're not married. I mean—a wife could help you steer—and things—while you sleep.
COACH. When I want to sleep, I just lash the wheel.
MISS BROOKS. Yes, but she could prepare well-balanced meals, and bring you cups of hot chocolate.
COACH. Meals! As soon as I get out of the tourist belt I buy stalks of bananas and hang them around in the rigging. Anytime I want a banana—[*Gestures.*]—I reach out. Then I get baskets of mangoes, and guavas and oranges. In the morning I cut myself a big slice of ripe papaya and squeeze fresh lime juice all over it. [*Accompanies this last with an imaginary*

squeezing of a lime. MISS BROOKS *involuntarily copies gesture.*]

TED [*without turning*]. Mmmmmmmmm . . .

COACH [*rising*]. Talk about a vacation . . . [*Looks front.*] First, you breathe all that clean salt air. Then a little rain squall sweeps over one of those green islands and blows out to you. [*Inhales deeply.*] It's like—gardenias. [MISS BROOKS, *gazing ahead of her, inhales it, too.* COACH *becomes all business again.*] Say, I better get back to the gym. You'll send Ted along soon——[MISS BROOKS *is still looking off.*] Miss Brooks!

MISS BROOKS [*starting*]. What?

COACH. You'll send Ted along soon?

MISS BROOKS. Ted? [*Recalls.*] Oh.

COACH. Basketball practice.

MISS BROOKS [*squinting at blackboard*]. He shouldn't be much longer.

COACH [*almost surprised*]. I certainly enjoyed talking to you. I hope we get another chance.

MISS BROOKS [*gathering up travel folders and dropping them in wastebasket*]. We will.

[SYLVIA, *a student, enters* R.]

SYLVIA. Miss Brooks—are you casting the play now?

MISS BROOKS. No, I'm not—thank heaven. [COACH *crosses past* SYLVIA.]

COACH. Excuse me. [*Goes out* R.]

SYLVIA. But I was told it was switched back to you.

MISS BROOKS. It wasn't.

SYLVIA. Oh. [*Goes out* R.]

MISS BROOKS [*happily, rising*]. What a relief—not having to battle over the play. [*Sighs.*] Now I'm going to enjoy *not* fighting with the coach!

TED. Is it as indescribable as that scenery in the wastebasket?

MISS BROOKS [*good-humoredly*]. Oh, shut up! [*Looks toward*

R, *thoughtfully.*] I think maybe I'll come along with Jane sometime soon and watch basketball practice.

TED. You know—on a little sailboat—I bet the odds are almost as good as in Alaska.

MISS BROOKS [*grimly, moving toward him*]. You're not only a copier—you're an eavesdropper.

TED [*shrugging*]. One thing leads to another. Would you like me to start another sentence?

MISS BROOKS. I'd like you to go to basketball practice.

TED. I think maybe I'll try out for the play.

MISS BROOK. Don't be silly. [*Crosses back to desk.*]

TED [*indignantly*]. What's so silly about it?

MISS BROOKS. I don't know—offhand. [*Concerned.*] The coach wouldn't like it. [*Sits at desk again.*]

TED [*starting to erase blackboard*]. Pretty soon I'll be graduating. The coach has to learn to get along without me. [MISS BROOKS *smiles and shakes her head at this.*]

[MR. WADSWORTH, *the principal, enters* R, *followed by* DORIS, *a student.* MISS BROOKS *gets right up.*]

MR. WADSWORTH [*with an edge in his voice*]. Miss Brooks——

MISS BROOKS [*respectfully*]. Yes, Mr. Wadsworth?

MR. WADSWORTH [*pausing at* R C]. I . . . [*Hesitates, as he becomes aware of the now madly erasing* TED]. What's he doing?

MISS BROOKS. Erasing the blackboard.

MR. WADSWORTH. I can see that.

MISS BROOKS [*looking for a legitimate "out" for* TED]. If he erases the blackboard, he's helping me tidy up the classroom. [*Decisively*]. He's helping me tidy up the classroom.

MR. WADSWORTH. That's Ted Wilder.

MISS BROOKS. Yes, Mr. Wadsworth.

MR. WADSWORTH [*testily, coming toward* MISS BROOKS' *desk*]. Did you have to pick out an important member of the basketball team?

MISS BROOKS. I'm sorry.

MR. WADSWORTH. You're always making mistakes like that.

DORIS [*tugging at him*]. Mr. Wadsworth . . .

MR. WADSWORTH [*irritated*]. You're always making—difficulties.

DORIS [*tugging at him again*]. Mr. Wadsworth . . .

MR. WADSWORTH. And another thing—— [*But he is diverted by the tugging.*] What is it?

DORIS. The school bus. [MR. WADSWORTH *assumes an attitude of patient listening.*] It keeps coming earlier and earlier. I think you should speak to the driver.

MR. WADSWORTH [*patiently*]. The bus is too early. I'll speak to the driver.

MISS BROOKS. If you want to speak to me about the contest, there's no question who wrote the best theme.

MR. WADSWORTH [*with faint acidity*]. I'm glad your decision was such an easy one. I want to see you about the school play.

MISS BROOKS. Miss Audubon is taking care of that. She's casting today.

MR. WADSWORTH [*to* DORIS]. Run along. [*As he continues on to* MISS BROOKS, DORIS *takes a reluctant step away from him.*] I happened to look in on the casting. Usually on the day the class play's being cast, I go home. [*Regretfully.*] I should have gone home today.

MISS BROOKS. Any special trouble?

MR. WADSWORTH. Miss Audubon has two girls weeping already.

MISS BROOKS. Only one best role?

MR. WADSWORTH [*nodding*]. I think you'd better take over.

MISS BROOKS. With the girls?

MR. WADSWORTH. With the play. [*His irritation grows as he is aware of* DORIS *behind him.*] Will you please run along? [DORIS *takes another step away from him.*]

MISS BROOKS [*sincerely*]. Give Miss Audubon a little more time. I'm sure she'll do a splendid job.

MR. WADSWORTH. Miss Audubon was about to start weeping herself. [*Firmly.*] You've got to take over.

MISS BROOKS [*coming in front of her desk*]. I can't just take over like that.
MR. WADSWORTH. Why can't you?
MISS BROOKS. For one thing, I don't have the extra time.
TED [*helpfully*]. Besides, she promised to come out and root for the basketball team.
MR. WADSWORTH. Basketball?
MISS BROOKS. What's so wrong about that?
MR. WADSWORTH [*with touch of severity*]. I'm sure the athletic director can manage without you.
MISS BROOKS [*woefully*]. I'm sure he can, too. Only——
MR. WADSWORTH. Only what?
MISS BROOKS. Only—[*With difficulty.*]—you see—the coach and I——
MR. WADSWORTH. Now don't worry about the use of the gymnasium. We can divide the time. There's *no* reason why you and the coach shouldn't get along fine.
MISS BROOKS [*apprehensively*]. But there will be. If I have to put on the play, there will. Please, Mr. Wadsworth!
MR. WADSWORTH. If you run into difficulties, I can straighten them out.
MISS BROOKS. But I don't want to run into difficulties—[*Glances R.*]—not with him!
MR. WADSWORTH. Now you're being unco-operative.
MISS BROOKS [*quickly*]. Mr. Wadsworth—I've so many papers to mark. [*Crosses behind desk, starts pulling piles of papers from her desk.*] Papers—endless papers. And I just finished judging the "Best Theme" contest. I have to judge a debate Friday, and chaperon two dances next week alone. Then more papers to mark——
MR. WADSWORTH [*directly in front of her desk, DORIS tagging after him*]. I suppose you think I have an easy time? Problems all day—and the minute I get home, the phone starts ringing. [*Imitates.*] It looks like snow, will there be school tomorrow? Can I have the keys to the gymnasium? Who's responsible for Albert not doing better in mathematics? The

Elks Club would like to use the music room. [*Turns to* DORIS, *slightly taken aback to find her right at his heels again.*] The bus was too early. [*Back to* MISS BROOKS.] Why don't we teach more about the Civil War?

MISS BROOKS [*stubbornly*]. Miss Audubon especially wanted to direct the play.

MR. WADSWORTH. Not any more.

MISS BROOKS. But she was so anxious——

MR. WADSWORTH. She's a talented music teacher, and I've decided it would be unwise to deprive the school band of her full time attention.

[STANLEY, *a student, enters* R.]

STANLEY [*in a complaining voice, coming to* R C]. Mr. Wadsworth . . .

MISS BROOKS. When did you reach this decision?

MR. WADSWORTH. It came to me while I was watching the tryouts.

MISS BROOKS. You're not giving Miss Audubon a fair chance. She's *very* talented. Remember the wonderful job she did with "The Pirates of Penzance"?—considering everything.

MR. WADSWORTH [*grimly*]. I remember.

STANLEY. Mr. Wadsworth . . .

MR. WADSWORTH [*finally turning, trying to keep his temper*]. What is it? [*Glares at* DORIS, *who is still at his heels, and she steps aside.*]

STANLEY. My mother said I was to speak to you about the school bus.

MR. WADSWORTH. Not now.

STANLEY. But my mother said so. [MR. WADSWORTH *sighs and assumes his attitude of patient listening.*] It keeps coming *later* and *later*. I think you should speak to the driver.

MR. WADSWORTH [*patiently*]. The bus is too late. I'll speak to the driver. [*Turns to* MISS BROOKS.]

STANLEY. Are the play tryouts going to be held here?

MISS BROOKS [*quickly*]. No.

MR. WADSWORTH [*just as quickly*]. Yes. You might pass the word. [STANLEY *nods and goes out* R.]

DORIS. The bus isn't too late. It's too early.

MR. WADSWORTH [*eyes heavenward*]. Yes. I'll speak to the driver. [*To* MISS BROOKS.] There's no one else. You've got to step in.

MISS BROOKS. Mr. Wadsworth. I have a reason—a personal reason——

MR. WADSWORTH. I should probably mention that Mrs. Allen—Mrs. Allen of the school board—recently drew attention to your lack of a Master's Degree.

MISS BROOKS. I'll bet it was recent—right after Rhonda Allen didn't win the "Best Theme" contest.

MR. WADSWORTH. We've an excellent board, and the majority agreed your work was quite satisfactory—especially when I pointed out how generously you give your time for student activities.

DORIS [*concerned*]. Don't you *want* to direct us in the play, Miss Brooks?

MISS BROOKS [*affectionately*]. Of course I *want* to, dear, but——

MR. WADSWORTH [*cutting in*]. Good! Then it's settled. [*Crosses toward* R *quickly.*]

MISS BROOKS [*hurrying after him*]. Just a minute!

MR. WADSWORTH [*bursting out*]. We'll hear no more discussion. You're insubordinate!

MISS BROOKS [*saluting him*]. Yes, General Eisenhower.

MR. WADSWORTH [*sharply*]. What did you say?

MISS BROOKS [*relaxing*]. I said—yes, I'll start this hour.

MR. WADSWORTH [*relaxing, too*]. Oh.

MISS BROOKS [*sighing, after pause*]. Could you help me work out the gymnasium problem with the coach? [*Hopefully.*] So there won't be grounds for any misunderstanding between us?

MR. WADSWORTH. There's nothing to it. You'll just have to see that the athletic program doesn't interfere with the play and the play doesn't interfere with athletics. [*Shrugs.*] It's so simple.

MISS BROOKS. But the trouble with that—you see——

MR. WADWORTH. I'd better explain things to Miss Audubon, and have them all come along in here.

MISS BROOKS [*helplessly*]. I don't even know what play was chosen.

MR. WADSWORTH [*confidently*]. You've nothing to worry about there. I picked it out myself.

MISS BROOKS. I hope it has an easy setting.

MR. WADSWORTH [*enthusiastically*]. A wonderful setting. The mountains of Tibet——

MISS BROOKS [*in horror*]. *Mountains of Tibet!*

MR. WADSWORTH [*nodding*]. Shangri-La. [*Takes copy of play from coat pocket.*] It's called "Lost Horizon."

DORIS. I saw the movie version. Gosh, was that a snowstorm!

MISS BROOKS [*her misery increasing*]. *Snowstorm!*

DORIS. And that airplane crash! [MISS BROOKS *looks at them, open-mouthed.*]

MR. WADSWORTH [*nodding*]. I remember the bells tolling—and Conway climbing up the mountain through the terrible blizzard——

MISS BROOKS [*weakly*]. You realize that all of this has to take place at the east end of our gymnasium?

MR. WADSWORTH [*handing her play*]. I'm sure it's all worked out in the book.

MISS BROOKS [*checking quickly*]. It calls for *seven men!*

MR. WADSWORTH. What of it?

MISS BROOKS. Seven parts for men. That means I'll have to find seven boys who aren't going out for basketball or baseball or intra-mural sports, or going bowling, or ice skating, or to the movies—who aren't too shy or busy, and happen to be interested in dramatics and this particular play, and the particular rôle in the particular play, and . . . [*Pauses for a breath.*]

MR. WADSWORTH [*shrugging*]. Some things you'll have to solve for yourself. [*Reading.*] I'll never forget the impression it all made on me. Take the character of Conway——

MISS BROOKS. The way I remember—that part calls for a disillusioned British diplomat. Who do you have in mind from among this student body to play a disillusioned British diplomat?

TED [*coming downstage, with his best English accent*]. I say, old girl—I'd rather like to take a crack at it.

MISS BROOKS [*giving him a look, turning to* MR. WADSWORTH]. Couldn't we just put on something simple and fun—for all girls?

MR. WADSWORTH [*the matter is closed*]. I'll have Miss Audubon send in everyone who's reported there. [*Starts* R.]

MISS BROOKS [*sighing*]. The weeping prima donnas.

MR. WADSWORTH [*hesitating*]. I understand Rhonda Allen is trying out.

MISS BROOKS [*this is a matter of principle*]. Well!

MR. WADSWORTH [*quickly*]. Nothing. Nothing at all.

MISS BROOKS. I wish you'd hold them off a few minutes—while I look over the play.

MR. WADSWORTH [*since it concerns him*]. Miss Brooks—for once I'd like a play put on at this school without any trouble or difficulties.

MISS BROOKS [*numbly*]. Yes, Mr. Wadsworth. No troubles or difficulties.

MR. WADSWORTH. And I want you to get along with the athletics director this time. I don't want to be called in every afternoon to settle arguments.

MISS BROOKS. I'll try my best. [*Fervently.*] Honestly—I'll try my best!

MR. WADSWORTH [*glowing*]. Now you're beginning to sound a little co-operative. [*Goes out* R.]

TED [*the moment* MR. WADSWORTH *is out the door, in mock gruff voice*]. Miss Brooks—I don't want any troubles or difficulties.

MISS BROOKS. You go to basketball practice. [*Crosses* U R C.]

I've got to skim this play. [*As she goes out* U R C.] Suiry, Jane—I need the office now. [*Goes out* U R C.]

[JANE *comes in* U R C.]

JANE. Thanks for letting me use your typewriter.

TED [*with his English accent*]. Been doing a spot of writing, what?

JANE [*bewildered*]. What?

DORIS [*admiringly*]. He's acting.

JANE [*coming to* R C]. Oh. [*After pause.*] What are you acting?

TED [*crossing to her*]. Characterization, old girl. I'm creating a character.

DORIS [*seriously*]. That's true. He's a character. [*Sits at one of desks.*]

JANE [*with a smile*]. He certainly is.

TED [*smiling*]. Hey—take it easy!

JANE [*noticing blackboard*]. I see you finished.

TED [*nodding*]. My debt to society.

JANE [*seriously*]. Just because Rhonda Allen practically held out her paper—you didn't have to copy. [TED *shakes his head.* JANE *speaks unhappily.*] If you *had* to copy, why didn't you look at *my* paper?

TED. I noticed you.

JANE [*pleased*]. You did?

TED [*nodding*]. All hunched up over it, like a strong wind was blowing.

JANE [*defensively*]. I didn't notice you noticed me. Maybe if I'd noticed——

TED [*regarding her*]. I know where else I've seen you—the lunchroom.

DORIS. Naturally. She dips the mashed potatoes on to the saucers, and puts cole slaw in the little plates.

TED. I guess I ought to thank you. I mean, those are really big helpings of cole slaw.

JANE [*uneasily, passing it off*]. There's no use letting it go to waste. [*With a nervous shrug, moving toward* L C.] I just happen to be a person who hates to see cole slaw wasted.

DORIS. I bet that isn't the real reason.

TED [*crossing toward* JANE]. What is?

DORIS [*as* JANE *looks horrified*]. School spirit. After all—the basketball team.

JANE [*with quick agreement*]. Yes.

TED [*a little disappointed*]. Anyway—thanks for the big helpings.

JANE [*earnestly*]. You're welcome! I'd make the servings lots bigger, only—[*Depreciating.*]—those little plates.

DORIS. She sure has school spirit.

TED [*thoughtfully*]. She sure has. [JANE *is embarrassed.*]

[MARGE, ELSIE, *and* SYLVIA *enter* R. *They move to* C *stage.*]

SYLVIA [*as she enters*]. First I was told it was *not* here. Now they say it's here again.

ELSIE. I was told the same thing.

MARGE [*with mock seriousness*]. Maybe it's a plot.

SYLVIA. Nothing that happens at this institution would surprise me.

ELSIE. People sometimes do things when other people are trying out for a play. [*Confidentially.*] You know how people are.

MARGE [*still not serious*]. Terrible!

ELSIE [*to* TED]. What are you doing here?

TED. A private matter between me and Miss Brooks.

ELSIE. Won't the coach be missing you?

TED [*shrugging*]. He'll have to manage somehow.

[FAITH *enters* R. *She has a handkerchief in her hand, which she has up to her face. She hurries to the chair* D R *and sits with her face averted.*]

MARGE [*with a meaning look at* FAITH]. Casting the play—what fun! What deep-down fun!

[ELAINE *enters* R. *She, also, has a handkerchief to her face, and crosses to sit in the chair right of the door* U R C.]

MARGE. What a jolly spirit of friendly rivalry.

FAITH. What a rotten exhibition of favoritism.

ELAINE. It isn't fair. [*Gulps.*]

[RHONDA ALLEN *enters* R *and pauses in the doorway to survey the scene.*]

MARGE [*pretending to be impressed*]. Imagine—Rhonda Allen —in person! [*To* OTHERS.] The rest of us might as well go home.

RHONDA [*coming into room to* C]. If there's one thing I hate it's petty jealousy.

FAITH. Miss Audubon *was* showing favoritism.

ELAINE. You didn't even read a line, and she gave you the best part.

RHONDA. Maybe she knew what she was doing.

MARGE. I'm sure.

RHONDA. What do you mean?

MARGE [*mockingly*]. Miss Allen—do you think if I used the same kind of soap you use for fourteen days I could be beautiful and successful like you are?

RHONDA. That's expecting a lot from a cake of soap.

MARGE [*innocently*]. Maybe if I used the same kind of soap your mother uses——

RHONDA [*shrugging*]. A little soap wouldn't hurt you. [*To* TED.] Hello, Ted.

TED [*waving to her*]. Hi!

RHONDA [*crossing to him*]. You came to watch me try out?

TED. Sure.

RHONDA. That's sweet.

DORIS [*rising*]. Excuse us!

SYLVIA. Maybe we're in the way!

ELSIE. Hey—no one brought the playbooks.

JANE [*unhappy at sight of* RHONDA *and* TED]. I'll get them. [*Hurries out* R.]

RHONDA [*to* TED]. You're missing basketball? [TED *nods.*]
SYLVIA. The coach is managing without him. [*Sits at one of desks.*]
MARGE [*also sitting at one of desks*]. Somehow.
ELSIE. What I want to know—do the tryouts start from the beginning, or from where Miss Audubon left off?
ELAINE. It's only fair to start from the beginning.
RHONDA. I don't see the point.
FAITH. You wouldn't.

[MISS BROOKS *has entered* U R C. *She has an open playbook and a piece of paper in her hand. She comes to* R C.]

DORIS [*seeing her*]. Hello, Miss Brooks.
GENERAL [*babble of voices, simultaneously*]. We were told to come here. Mr. Wadsworth told us. You're supposed to direct the play. We're supposed to try out now. I'm glad it's you, Miss Brooks. What part can I have? Can I be in the play? I think it's a wonderful play! Please, Miss Brooks, can I play an older woman? [*They surround her at* R C.]
MISS BROOKS. Quiet! [*Holds up her hands.*] Quiet! [*As they subside. Nods towards* R.] You'll be disturbing the basketball team. [*Crosses* L, *reaches into her desk, and takes out a box of Kleenex.*] Before we have any tryouts, I've got something for all of you. [*Crosses and hands box to* SYLVIA.] Here, Sylvia—I want you to pass out one to each. [SYLVIA *passes one tissue to each as* MISS BROOKS *continues. Then she leaves box on* MISS BROOKS' *desk.*] *None* of you is going to get the part you want. You're *all* going to be terribly disappointed and want to cry your eyes out. If any of you need any more Kleenex, feel perfectly free to help yourselves. There's no charge. [*There are smiles from* ALL. *She continues.*] Now—I want all the girls to line up on this side. [*Gestures* R, *and* GIRLS *move* R.] Come along now. And all the boys ... [*Hesitates, as shifting* GIRLS *reveal just* TED. *Her voice slows to a halt.*] And—all—the ...
TED [*nodding*]. Just me.

MISS BROOKS. You should be in the gym.

TED. I'm trying out.

MISS BROOKS. Yes, but . . . [*Hesitates, then addresses* GIRLS.] Didn't *any* other boys report for the tryout? [*There is a general shaking of heads.*]

DORIS. I think maybe Stanley will come—only I'm not sure. [MISS BROOKS *looks hopelessly at her playbook, and then back at the assemblage.*]

TED. It looks like I don't have much competition.

MISS BROOKS. It looks like it.

TED [*nodding in a satisfied manner*]. It looks like I get the lead——

MISS BROOKS [*looking at her paper*]. That would be Conway—"a tall, bronzed Englishman, inclined to look brooding until he smiles. He is a brilliant, though disillusioned member of the British Foreign Service."

TED [*confidently*]. That's me.

MISS BROOKS [*worried*]. Won't this interfere with basketball? After all, the coach may need you.

TED. Don't worry. I can still play the games, and get plenty of practice, too.

MISS BROOKS. Yes, but the coach may feel——

TED. I'll explain to him.

RHONDA. Besides, you don't have anyone else.

MISS BROOKS [*unhappily*]. No.

RHONDA. Having Ted play Conway—[*Delighted.*]—that'll be perfect!

MISS BROOKS [*to* TED]. You're sure it won't interfere?

TED. Absolutely.

MISS BROOKS [*sighing*]. I *hope* not.

[JANE *enters* R *with the playbooks.*]

JANE. The copies of the play, Miss Brooks. [*Crosses to her at* C *stage.*]

MISS BROOKS. Oh. Thank you, Jane. Would you hand them out?

[JANE *passes out playbooks as scene continues.*] There now—you're fully equipped.

TED [*to* JANE]. One for me, too. I'm playing Conway.

JANE. You are? [TED *nods.*]

RHONDA [*possessively*]. And I'm Helen.

JANE [*swallowing*]. Oh. [*Hands* TED *a playbook.*]

MISS BROOKS [*to* RHONDA]. There's still a formality of trying out for the part.

RHONDA. Miss Audubon already gave it to me.

MISS BROOKS [*holding her patience*]. I'm afraid it's my responsibility now.

RHONDA. What have you got against me?

MISS BROOKS. Not a thing, Rhonda dear. Won't you be the first to try for the part?

RHONDA. Maybe it's better to be the last.

MISS BROOKS. All right, then. Be last.

RHONDA [*quickly*]. No, I'll be first.

MISS BROOKS [*at* C *stage*]. I've just skimmed through the play, but I remember the story. Turn to page one hundred and eleven. Conway has come to this wonderful, peaceful place called Shangri-La, but his companion is urging him to leave. [JANE *joins the other* GIRLS *as* ALL *open playbooks.*] The ruler, who they call the High Lama, has died, and they've asked Conway to rule in his place. The very beautiful Helen, who lives there, is *begging* Conway to stay at Shangri-La. Now try it, Rhonda.

RHONDA [*stepping forward, reading from her playbook; she reads too fast, and in a singsong fashion*]. "You've got to stay, Conway. Shangri-La belongs to you. The High Lama saw something in you that——"

MISS BROOKS [*cutting in*]. Not so fast, Rhonda. You're pleading with this man to stay.

RHONDA [*in exactly the same manner*]. "You've got to stay, Conway. Shangri-La belongs to you. The——"

MISS BROOKS. Rhonda—you're *begging* him—for his own good,

and because you're fond of him. Try it slowly. Take it a little further on.

RHONDA [*in the same manner, though louder*]. "You belong here, and I want you to stay, too."

MISS BROOKS [*reading*]. He says, "Helen."

TED [*saying it*]. "Helen."

MISS BROOKS [*reading*]. "She kisses him lightly and says, 'Don't go.'"

RHONDA. "Don't go." [*Woodenly, as before.*] "I want you to stay."

MISS BROOKS. Thank you, Rhonda. [*Phrases it carefully.*] I'm sure—with practice—I mean, I'm sure with *enough* practice, you'll do very well.

SYLVIA [*at this apparent favoritism*]. Oh—boy!

MARGE. How wonderful—to be Rhonda Allen!

RHONDA [*pleased, crossing and taking* TED'S *arm*]. Then it's settled?

MISS BROOKS [*nodding*]. If no one else wishes to try out for this role . . . [*Relieved that no one speaks. Continues quickly.*] We'll get on to the other parts.

JANE [*who has been watching* RHONDA *with* TED, *bursting out*]. Miss Brooks! [*Steps forward.*]

MISS BROOKS [*continuing*]. The other parts are quite interesting, and——

JANE. Miss Brooks!

MISS BROOKS [*pausing*]. Yes?

JANE [*swallowing*]. I—could *I* try out—reading the part of Helen?

MISS BROOKS [*not wanting trouble*]. Jane—considering everything—I really think——

TED. It wouldn't hurt to give her a chance. [*There is a murmur of approval, except from* RHONDA.] It's supposed to be a tryout. [RHONDA *darts an angry glance at* TED, *and removes her arm. She moves* D L.]

MISS BROOKS. Of course. Any one of you is welcome to try. [JANE *is looking at* TED.] Well—go ahead.

JANE. Yes. [*Looks down at playbook and then back to* TED. *She speaks slowly, with proper emphasis and with obvious feeling.*] "You've got to stay, Conway. Shangri-La belongs to you." [*Looks at playbook again, then back at* TED.] "The High Lama saw something in you that made him feel you were the person to lead us. I think I see it, too. And—[*Fervently.*]— I want you to stay." [*Crosses close to* TED.]

MISS BROOKS [*gently, reading*]. He says, "Helen."

TED [*gently*]. "Helen."

MISS BROOKS [*reading*]. "She kisses him lightly and says, 'Don't go!'"

JANE [*actually kissing* TED *lightly, speaking in a low voice*]. "Don't go." [*There is a pause. The* OTHERS *are impressed by* JANE, *who puts her playbook down, and steps back, intensely embarrassed. Someone lets out a low whistle.*]

MISS BROOKS [*finally breaking pause*]. Does anyone else want to try out for the part of Helen? [*There is a shaking of heads all down the line at* R *stage.*]

RHONDA. You're *not* going to give her that part?

FAITH. *You're* not the director.

ELAINE. It's up to Miss Brooks.

DORIS. I think Jane was very good.

RHONDA. You already gave her the "Best Theme" award.

SYLVIA. Maybe it was the best theme.

MARGE. It was sure the best reading.

TED. If you want *my* opinion——

MISS BROOKS. I don't.

RHONDA. She's your favorite, that's all.

MARGE [*mocking*]. If there's one thing I hate, it's petty jealousy.

MISS BROOKS. That's enough, Margaret. And it's enough from you, too, Rhonda.

RHONDA. Do I get the part?

MISS BROOKS [*the problem has her a little confused*]. I—uh— I——

RHONDA [*her most crushing argument*]. My mother especially wants me in the play.

MISS BROOKS [*after a pause, as this makes up her mind*]. And you'll *be* in the play, Rhonda.[*Takes a breath.*] But I think we'll try Jane in the part of Helen. [*From the others there is a suppressed reaction of surprise and pleasure at* MISS BROOKS' *decision.* MISS BROOKS *continues quickly.*] There are lots of wonderful parts in this play! [*Looks at her paper.*] Two attractive English girls—Lo-Tsen, the exquisite Chinese girl —Miss Brinklow, a missionary, and it's a real acting opportunity. If we can't find a few more boys, some of their parts are going to be open, and they're all exceptional.

RHONDA. I don't want any part but Helen.

MISS BROOKS. Rhonda—please.

RHONDA. I don't care.

MISS BROOKS. But some of the other parts——

RHONDA [*her voice higher*]. I don't want any part but Helen.

MISS BROOKS [*to* OTHERS]. Why don't you study the play? [*There is a sudden fussing with playbooks. To* RHONDA.] I'm sorry.

RHONDA [*crossing to* MISS BROOKS]. I wouldn't care if you gave the part to anyone but her. It's just that I can't stand favoritism.

TED. Take it easy, Rhonda.

MISS BROOKS. It isn't a question of favoritism. It's a question of judgment.

RHONDA [*bitterly*]. I've heard that a Master's Degree is a real help to better judgment. [*Turns and starts R.*]

TED. Hey—Rhonda! [*But* RHONDA *puts her handkerchief to her face and hurries out* R. *The* OTHERS *are puzzled by what* RHONDA *has said.*]

MISS BROOKS [*answering them*]. She's disappointed, that's all. It's only natural.

TED. I'd say she was more burned up.

ELAINE [*not unhappily*]. Sizzling!

TED [*hoping to reassure* MISS BROOKS]. Maybe I can cool her off. Maybe I can even cool off her mother—[*Doubtfully.*]— maybe. [*Explaining.*] I have a date with Rhonda tonight.

FAITH. Her and her father's sports car.

TED [*with mock seriousness*]. Isn't that a beauty?

JANE [*unhappily*]. Miss Brooks—might as well let her have the part. [*With a quick glance at* TED, *discouraged.*] It doesn't make any difference.

MISS BROOKS [*firmly*]. Listen to me, Jane. You've got the part and you'd better be a credit to my—judgment. [*Shakes her head.*] Now we'll get along with the tryouts—if there aren't any more objections.

[*There is a murmur of agreement from the* OTHERS, *which is cut off as the door* R *bursts open and the* COACH *enters.*]

COACH [*sharply, pushing his way past the* GIRLS *to* C *stage*]. Miss Brooks. Where's Ted?

TED. Right here, Coach.

COACH [*to* TED]. Is she still keeping you?

TED. In a way—you see——

COACH [*turning to her, outraged*]. Miss Brooks!

MISS BROOKS. Just a moment. [*To* OTHERS.] We'll continue the tryouts at the east end of the gym. Go along and study your books.

COACH. There's basketball practice in the gym.

MISS BROOKS. I'm entitled to the east end. [*To* OTHERS.] Go along.

COACH. You stay here, Ted. [ALL, *except* TED, COACH, *and* MISS BROOKS *file out* R, *chatting noisily.*]

MISS BROOKS [*who has followed them to door* R]. We'll try it. If it's too noisy, we can come back here. I'll be there in a minute.

COACH [*when the commotion has subsided*]. Now—if you'll explain!

MISS BROOKS [*trying to calm him, moving to* R C]. Hugo— please——

COACH [*still sharp*]. I can't understand why you're still keeping Ted.

TED. She isn't—not exactly.

COACH. Then what are you doing?

TED. The play.

COACH [*in horror*]. The play!

MISS BROOKS. Ted decided to try out for the play.

COACH [*crossing to her*]. You didn't give him a part?

MISS BROOKS. Hugo—I have to find seven boys for the play.

COACH. You *don't* have to take the mainstay of the basketball team?

MISS BROOKS. I didn't suggest it.

COACH. But you got him anyway. [TED *nods.*] Of all the low-down tricks——

MISS BROOKS. He said it wouldn't matter. He said he could get in plenty of practice.

TED. Sure, Coach——

MISS BROOKS [*hopefully*]. I can arrange things on rehearsals.

TED. It'll work out swell. I play a disillusioned member of the British Foreign Service.

COACH. I'm getting pretty disillusioned myself. [*To* MISS BROOKS.] I certainly had the wrong impression of you.

MISS BROOKS. No other boys turned out for the play——

COACH. First, you kid me along, pretending you like sailing and the tropics.

MISS BROOKS [*eagerly*]. I do—at least, I'm certain.

COACH [*bitterly, moving* D R]. You get me thinking maybe it *would* be nice to have someone to help steer—[*Looks off.*] —and maybe fix cups of hot chocolate—[*Turns to* MISS BROOKS.]—then you do a trick like this.

MISS BROOKS. It's no trick——

COACH. I was right about you in the first place.

MISS BROOKS. You were not.

TED. You're all wrong, Coach.

COACH [*crying out, as he crosses to* TED]. Why would a healthy basketball player want to be a—a disillusioned member of the British Foreign Service? [TED *shakes his head.* COACH *looks sharply to* MISS BROOKS *for the answer, but she can only shrug helplessly. She doesn't know.*]

COACH. What am I going to do Saturday afternoon?

MISS BROOKS. I didn't mean to cause you any trouble.

COACH. It seems to me you used mighty poor judgment.

MISS BROOKS. There've been other complaints.

COACH. Ted—what are you going to do?

TED. I'll make twenty points Saturday, Coach. A few hours off for rehearsal won't hurt me. [*Notices* COACH *is about to explode.*] I better join the others. [*Hurries out* R.]

COACH. A few hours! [*Sinks down at one of desks.*] If I don't kick him off the team, what'll happen to discipline? [MISS BROOKS *shakes her head.*] And if I do kick him off, what'll happen to the team? [MISS BROOKS *shakes her head again.*] You!

MISS BROOKS [*moving toward him*]. Please, Hugo!

COACH. And just a short while ago, I was thinking you—that you——

MISS BROOKS. Yes?

COACH. Ha! [*Angrily, rises.*] I'm going to make certain you don't get an unfair amount of gym time.

MISS BROOKS [*getting angry herself*]. Don't try to take it *all*—like you did last year.

COACH. Like *I* did!

MISS BROOKS. It seems to me you're being ridiculous. Just because one of your athletes would rather be in the play—it doesn't give you grounds to jump to conclusions about a person.

COACH [*pacing to* R C]. I'm not jumping to conclusions.

MISS BROOKS. You certainly are.

COACH. How about that poor little girl I passed in the hall—the one that came away from here weeping? I suppose she was jumping to conclusions, too.

MISS BROOKS. You don't understand.

COACH. I'm beginning to.

[MISS AUDUBON *enters* L.]

MISS AUDUBON [*very irritated*]. I thought you'd be casting in here. [*Comes downstage of* MISS BROOKS' *desk.*]

COACH. She's using part of *my* gym.

MISS BROOKS. I'm awfully sorry, Miss Audubon.

MISS AUDUBON [*bringing over some papers she carries*]. Since you had the play taken away from me, you might as well have my notes, too. [*Hands her papers.*]

COACH [*his horror at her increasing, crossing to* MISS BROOKS]. Had the play taken *away* from Miss Audubon!

MISS BROOKS. I didn't. It's just that Mr. Wadsworth felt band practice was so important—it should have your full attention.

MISS AUDUBON. I only have a few for band practice. Don't think you're fooling me——

COACH [*as* MISS BROOKS *turns to him*]. Or me——

MISS AUDUBON [*as* MISS BROOKS *turns to her*]. Going behind my back——

MISS BROOKS. Miss Audubon——

COACH [*dumbfounded*]. Going behind *her* back! [*Points off* R.] Making that little girl weep! Tricking me out of my athletes! I'm glad I found out about you! [*Starts for the door* R.]

MISS BROOKS [*taking a step after him*]. Hugo . . . [COACH *stalks out* R.]

MISS AUDUBON. I don't know what you said to Mr. Wadsworth, but it certainly worked wonders.

MISS BROOKS. Wonders?

MISS AUDUBON. You got the play again. You win. I hope you're happy.

MISS BROOKS. Me, happy—because of the play?

MISS AUDUBON. Of course. *You win!* [*Goes out* L, *sniffing audibly.* MISS BROOKS *looks after her dolefully for a minute. She sighs, crosses to her desk, reaches down into wastebasket and pulls out travel folders again.*]

[MISS FINCH *hurries in* R.]

MISS FINCH [*coming in front of* MISS BROOKS' *desk*]. Mr. Wadsworth sent me down. He said I should remind you to take care of getting the tickets printed. Attractive, but inexpensive. He wants you to take care of the setting, too—make it colorful and appropriate, but check any expenses with him. Then there's the question of the program, and selling advertising for it—make costumes, collect the necessary properties, and so forth. Am I boring you? [MISS BROOKS *shakes her head dumbly.*] Another thing—just as I left, Rhonda Allen came charging into his office. Does that mean anything? [MISS BROOKS *nods.*] What? [MISS BROOKS *shakes her head.*] What's happened?

MISS BROOKS. Nothing. [*Indicates travel folders, and swallows miserably.*] A person could waste two hundred and thirty-five dollars on a trip like this?

MISS FINCH [*surprised*]. Waste?

MISS BROOKS [*nodding unhappily*]. You know what those banana ports are like! [MISS FINCH *shakes her uncomprehending head. The band, loud and off key, starts up in the next room, off* L.]

MISS FINCH [*at the sound*]. Oh, no!

MISS BROOKS [*grimly*]. Oh, yes. [*Sighs.*] I better get on with the casting.

[*A* BASKETBALL PLAYER, *wearing his outfit and bouncing a basketball before him, comes in* R *and circles* MISS BROOKS, *bouncing the ball as he does.* NOTE: *If extra boys are available, a group of them could come in, passing the ball back and forth, and shouting at one another.* MISS FINCH *jumps out of the way.*]

BASKETBALL PLAYER. Don't mind me, Miss Brooks. [*As he bounces ball.*] The coach said if you were going to use part of the gym, we'd use part of the English room. [*Curtain starts down.*]

MISS BROOKS [*throwing travel folders back into wastebasket, unhappily.*] I win! [*Starts for door* R. MISS FINCH *starts to follow. The* BASKETBALL PLAYER *keeps bouncing ball as he moves toward* MISS FINCH. *One bounce comes too close to* MISS FINCH'S *heels for comfort, and she gives a little shriek, quickening her pace as she goes out after* MISS BROOKS.]

CURTAIN

ACT TWO

AT RISE OF CURTAIN: *The scene is the same, several weeks later. A quantity of material has been assembled for the production of "Lost Horizon," and is stacked at the left side of the classroom. There should be enough, perhaps including several flats for the set, so that it definitely fills up that side of the room. If possible, a large and colorful array should be assembled here.* ELSIE *is knee-deep in the material, shifting things about as she looks for something.* SYLVIA *is standing by with a check list on a clip board. At R stage, working on a stand which holds a spotlight, are* STANLEY *and* MARTIN. STANLEY *is on the floor checking a wire connection, while* MARTIN *watches the spotlight for any sign of life.*]

STANLEY [*hopefully*]. Is it on now?

MARTIN. No.

STANLEY [*pointing along electric line to the spotlight, then up the stand, and slowly does an imaginary "switch-on" of light*]. It *must* be on. [MARTIN *turns spot down towards* STANLEY. STANLEY *speaks as if making a great discovery.*] Something is wrong!

MARTIN [*pantomiming applause for this brilliance*]. We better leave it for Miss Brooks.

ELSIE. Here they are [*Picks up two Chinese lanterns.*] Two Chinese lanterns.

SYLVIA [*marking her paper*]. Check.

ELSIE [*looking closer*]. One of them has a tear. [*Gets up.*] Maybe Miss Brooks knows how to mend it. What's next?

SYLVIA. A bicycle. [*Turns.*] Hey, Stanley—you're supposed to leave your bicycle here till after the play.

STANLEY. I *need* my bicycle.

SYLVIA. Miss Brooks says it's required.

STANLEY [*puzzled*]. Did they have bicycles at Shangri-La?
SYLVIA [*gesturing towards* MARTIN]. Ask the High Lama.
MARTIN [*striking a pose, over-acting*]. "My son—we must keep safe the treasures of civilization behind the mountains of Shangri-La." [*Gestures.*] And what treasure of civilization compares with your bicycle?
STANLEY [*seriously*]. You think that's why she wants it?
MARTIN [*himself again*]. How do I know? Just go get it. [*Shaking his head,* STANLEY *goes out* R.]
ELSIE [*to* MARTIN]. I'm surprised you took time from basketball to be in the play.
MARTIN [*ruefully*]. Ted talked me into it.
SYLVIA. What'd he say?
MARTIN. He mentioned the great need for someone to play the High Lama. After that, he mentioned what a wonderful acting opportunity it is. Then he went on to say that if I didn't try out he'd kick my teeth in.
SYLVIA. Very persuasive.
MARTIN. Anyway—[*Dusts off his coat.*]—I was going to try out for the play, anyway.

[DORIS *enters* L, *carrying as many boxes of soap flakes as she can manage.*]

DORIS. This was all I could get. [*Dumps them at* L *stage.*]
SYLVIA [*checking her list*]. Soap flakes.
ELSIE. How come soap flakes?
SYLVIA [*shrugging*]. How come a bicycle?
DORIS. I saved the bill. [*Holds up slip.*]
SYLVIA. Collect from Miss Brooks.
DORIS. I saw Jane in the hall. She was trying to look as though nothing happened.
ELSIE. How's she supposed to look?
DORIS. She got fired from her lunchroom job.
SYLVIA. We heard. Somebody reported she was dishing out unequal portions—playing favorites.
ELSIE [*nodding*]. Favorites. Ted Wilder.

DORIS. They should consider all she's doing for the play.
SYLVIA [*looking at her list*]. Now you're supposed to get a big piece of tin from the janitor.
DORIS [*startled*]. A big piece of tin?
SYLVIA. Hurry up. [DORIS *sighs and hurries out* L.]
MARTIN. Why should Ted Wilder be entitled to special consideration?
ELSIE [*to* MARTIN]. No one said he is. You better get those lights set up.
MARTIN [*taking out a paper, indignantly*]. That's easy to say. [*Crosses toward* SYLVIA *and* ELSIE.] Look at the list! Footlights, border lights, spotlights, strip lights—Miss Brooks will have to take over. *I'm* no electrician.
SYLVIA [*sarcastically*]. It's a good thing Miss Brooks is an electrician.
MARTIN [*crossing back, fussing with spotlight again*]. I'm doing the best I can.
ELSIE [*to* SYLVIA]. Who do you suppose did report Jane?
SYLVIA [*shaking head*]. Making a person lose her job—that's a low-down trick.

[MARGE *has entered* L, *carrying a large cardboard box.*]

MARGE. I got the drapes, but someone will have to sew on the hooks.
SYLVIA. Who'd you have in mind?
MARGE [*shrugging*]. Maybe Miss Brooks. [*Dumps box at* L *stage.*]
SYLVIA [*marking her list again*]. I'll tell her.

[ELAINE *and* FAITH *enter* R.]

ELAINE. Where's Miss Brooks?
SYLVIA. Still working on stage.
FAITH [*crossing to* C *with* ELAINE]. We're going to speak to her about our parts. We don't get to wear any costumes. Maybe Miss Brooks could re-write them a little.

ELAINE. It isn't fair. Did you see the costume Rhonda Allen gets to swank around in?

SYLVIA. So her mother sent to New York——

MARGE. It helps convince Rhonda that Lo-Tsen is the best part in the play—and everybody's happy.

ELAINE. I'm not happy.

FAITH. Neither am I—and I'm going to take it up with Miss Brooks.

SYLVIA. It looks like a number of things are going to be taken up with Miss Brooks.

[JANE *enters* R. *She is dressed in old dungarees and an older sweater. She carries a pail of paint, and several brushes.*]

FAITH. I thought the painting was all finished.

JANE [*coming to* R C]. Not quite.

SYLVIA [*hesitating*]. I heard about the lunchroom——

JANE [*passing it off*]. I have more time for the play. [*Thinking about it.*] And after the play—I just don't care about after.

ELSIE. I'd think you'd be worn out from work.

JANE. I've never had so much fun in my life. [*Seriously.*] I guess this is the most fun in my life.

[RHONDA *enters* R. *She has on an attractive Chinese kimono.* MARTIN *whistles appreciatively at her. She glances about the room.*]

RHONDA. Is rehearsal about to start? [*Comes to* R C.]

ELSIE. Soon, probably.

RHONDA. My mother's going to watch. [*To* JANE.] You must have finished up early at the lunchroom.

JANE [*nodding slowly*]. I finished up.

SYLVIA. You know she got fired. Somebody reported she was playing favorites.

RHONDA [*bitterly, to* JANE]. I saw you. When Ted held out his plate you gave him three Swiss steaks. Don't you think three Swiss steaks is being a little obvious?

ELSIE [*to* RHONDA]. I bet it was you!

JANE [*in low voice, speaking carefully*]. I like Ted. I guess it's a little obvious.

RHONDA [*to* JANE]. Remember, those lines you're saying to each other—they're just in the play. It's all over Saturday night.

JANE [*seriously*]. I'll remember. [*She can't help herself.*] But it won't ever be over—not for me. [*Suddenly embarrassed. Smiles nervously.*] Gosh, all this paint—I'm not getting *any* work done. [*Goes out* R, *hurriedly.*]

MARGE [*breaking the pause*]. The nice thing about you, Rhonda—you're so subtle. You're not at all obvious.

RHONDA [*changing subject, moving toward* L *stage*]. Thank you. My mother brought two authentic Chinese vases to decorate the stage.

MARGE. Any president of the school board is welcome to attend rehearsal on presentation of two authentic Chinese—[*Broad "a".*]—vases.

RHONDA [*as she starts out* L, *matching* MARGE'S *tone*]. I'll tell her. [*Goes out* L.]

ELSIE. Should I warn Miss Brooks?

SYLVIA [*shaking head*]. She wanted to finish painting before—[*Looks* R.]—basketball practice—[*Looks* L.]—before they strike up the band.

MARTIN [*who has been examining spotlight all this while*]. Maybe *this* is the trouble. [*Turns switch and a bright spot comes on. It is pointed directly at* L *door.*] Hey! [*Proudly.*] I fixed it!

[MRS. ALLEN *has entered* L *and stands blinking in the bright light. She is carrying two elaborate Chinese vases.* RHONDA *is standing behind her.*]

MRS. ALLEN. You're blinding me! Put out that light! [MARTIN *frantically grabs switch and shuts off light.* MRS. ALLEN *speaks sharply.*] I might have broken one of these vases. [*She uses broad "a."*]

MARTIN. I'm terribly sorry. It was an accident. Honestly——
MRS. ALLEN [*calmed*]. I was just startled, that's all.
MARGE [*wiping off a chair quickly at R stage and bringing it to C stage*]. Won't you sit down?
MRS. ALLEN [*still holding vases*]. Thank you. [*Sits.*]
SYLVIA [*moving toward her*]. I'm in charge of the props. [*Indicates vases.*] Would you like me to take those?
MRS. ALLEN [*shaking her head*]. Isn't Miss Brooks here to supervise? [*There is a general shaking of heads.*]
ELSIE. Not right now.
MARGE. She's doing some work on stage.

[STANLEY *enters R, wheeling his bicycle.*]

MRS. ALLEN [*looking about*]. This isn't a storeroom. It's a classroom. [STANLEY *wheels bicycle to L stage and props it against wall.*]
SYLVIA. The stage is next door. This is a very convenient location.
MRS. ALLEN. I see. [*Noticing.*] Why aren't the rest of you dressed for rehearsal? Rhonda's the only one who has her costume.
RHONDA [*moving toward her mother*]. Please, Mother.
MARGE [*carefully*]. The rest of us are working on the play in other ways, too—the setting, assembling the properties, things like that.
MRS. ALLEN [*to* RHONDA]. Then why aren't you helping? [ALL *watch intently.*]
RHONDA. I'm supposed to be an aristocratic Chinese girl, and aristocratic Chinese girls have very long fingernails. [*Holds out her hands.*] You wouldn't want me to break one? [OTHERS *wince at this excuse.*]
MARGE. The rest of us can manage the work, Mrs. Allen.

[MISS BROOKS *enters R. She is wearing work clothes—perhaps some old slacks and a man's shirt. If this is not practical, any other clothes that are obviously work clothes will do.*]

MRS. ALLEN. There's no reason why *any* of you should carry an unfair load. After all, the play is one of Miss Brooks' jobs. She gets paid for it.

MISS BROOKS [*coming into the room*]. She gets paid less than a dogcatcher. [*Comes to* R C.]

MRS. ALLEN. What was that?

MISS BROOKS [*lightly*]. I just said—less than a dogcatcher. [*Continues quickly.*] What a lovely pair of vases. [*Rhymes with "cases."*]

MRS. ALLEN. These vases—[*Broad "a."*]—will give a touch of authenticity to the setting.

MISS BROOKS. But they're too valuable.

MRS. ALLEN [*firmly*]. Miss Brooks, I've gone to a great deal of trouble.

MISS BROOKS. Of course—and you're very kind. Thank you, Mrs. Allen—[*Takes vases apprehensively.*]—on behalf of the entire cast. Elsie, dear—set them on my desk. [ELSIE *crosses to* MISS BROOKS. *Handling them gingerly,* ELSIE *takes two vases into* MISS BROOKS' *office* U R C.]

MRS. ALLEN. Your dress seems a little inappropriate for a teacher at this school.

MISS BROOKS. I don't wear it during school hours. [*Patiently.*] I've been painting flats.

MRS. ALLEN. Doesn't this clutter upset your classwork?

MISS BROOKS. A little.

MRS. ALLEN. I'm glad you put my vases in your office. [*Rises.*] If you won't be starting rehearsal for a while, I think I'll see Mr. Wadsworth.

[*There is a loud crash from* MISS BROOKS' *office, off* U R C. ALL *freeze with horror. After a pause, the door* U R C *opens, and* ELSIE *enters nervously.*]

ELSIE [*clearing her throat*]. When I put the vases on the desk —[*Swallows.* MISS BROOKS *shuts her eyes with pain.*]—I knocked over the flower jar—the one with the hyacinth. [*There is a general release and* ALL *take a breath.*]

MRS. ALLEN [*after breathing deeply*]. I *must* catch Mr. Wadsworth. [*Crosses* L.]

MISS BROOKS. Always nice to see you. [MRS. ALLEN *goes out* L. MISS BROOKS *turns and looks them over, letting out a sigh.*] Oh, Elsie!

ELSIE. I'm so sorry about the hyacinth.

MISS BROOKS. The hyacinth! [*Laughs weekly and shakes her head.*] You gave me such a scare! [*Then they descend on her. The following lines are given simultaneously, with the helpless* MISS BROOKS *in the middle of the uproar.*]

ELAINE. Miss Brooks—we want to talk to you about our parts.

FAITH. We're not entirely satisfied.

MARGE [*holding them up for inspection*]. Is this the right color for the drapes?

STANLEY. Miss Brooks—can I use my bicycle after rehearsal?

ELSIE. There's a tear in one of the lamps—[*Holds it towards her.*]—see?

SYLVIA [*waving it towards her.*] Miss Brooks—you better inspect the list!

MARTIN. Miss Brooks—about the lights—Miss Brooks——

MISS BROOKS [*throwing up her hands*]. All of you—*quiet!* [ALL *subside.*] I don't want any more outbursts.

ELAINE. Faith and I aren't satisfied with our parts. They aren't big enough.

MISS BROOKS. I'm afraid that means I'll have to find someone else.

FAITH [*shocked*]. No! We didn't mean *anything* like that!

ELAINE. Everyone in my family bought tickets.

MISS BROOKS. Then stop being so silly—and listen. I'm just a tired old English teacher, with troubles of my own. I wish you wouldn't add to my misery.

ELSIE. We didn't do anything.

MISS BROOKS. Someone was seen smoking in the hall after rehearsal, and it was brought to my attention—*forcefully*. Then someone got home extra late after rehearsal and told her mother she'd been kept here reading lines till midnight. That was also brought to my attention.

MARGE [*worried*]. You didn't say we got out at ten o'clock?

MISS BROOKS [*shaking head*]. I took the rap. But I'd like to mention that I manage to get into enough trouble all by myself—I don't require outside assistance. [*Crosses behind her desk.*]

SYLVIA. You mean—you and the coach?

MISS BROOKS [*mockingly*]. Yes, I mean me and the coach. [*Changes subject.*] This play goes on in a week. You'll all have to work harder.

RHONDA. I'm ready to go over and over my lines.

MISS BROOKS. I was thinking of less aesthetic tasks—such as lettering posters, getting ads for the program, setting up lights, locating furniture, painting flats. Jane and I can't do it all. How about the rest of you?

FAITH. We got dates and things.

ELAINE. What's a girl to do?

MISS BROOKS. Well, last night, I did the lay-out on the program, checked the prop list, made a cue sheet, and worked out some lighting problems. Then I made some coffee, and relaxed while I marked sixty-four English papers.

RHONDA. Well?

MISS BROOKS Maybe I'd rather have been out on a date myself.

ELSIE [*shocked*]. You?

SYLVIA. On a *date?*

FAITH. You're over thirty!

MISS BROOKS. Medical science is advancing so fast, I may have two or three more useful years.

RHONDA. I bet it's the coach.

MARGE [*severely*]. You won't get anywhere, if you keep fighting with him.

SYLVIA. According to a column in the newspaper, you have to be interested in a man's hobbies.

MISS BROOKS. Thanks—I read the same column.

MARGE. But you keep on fighting.

ELSIE [*reciting*]. "You should demonstrate genuine knowledge of his favorite subject, and ask his opinion about it."

MISS BROOKS [*with mock severity*]. I think it's high time this class was graduated. [*Firmly.*] Now, do you mind if we get back to rehearsal?

[DORIS *enters* L, *carrying a big piece of tin.*]

DORIS. Here it is. But what is it? [*Crosses to* MISS BROOKS.]

MISS BROOKS. For the play.

SYLVIA. Miss Brooks—all these things. Maybe if we knew what they were for——

ELSIE. *Why* soap flakes? *Why* pieces of tin?

STANLEY. My bicycle?

MISS BROOKS. Sound effects.

RHONDA. Most schools use sound-effect records.

MISS BROOKS. Most schools allow funds for such purposes.

MARGE. What kind of sound effects?

MISS BROOKS [*holding out her hands*]. Give me that, Doris. [*Takes tin from* DORIS, *and then turns to* OTHERS.] You might as well see. Stanley, put your bike on its stand and start pumping. [STANLEY *sets his bicycle up at* C *stage*. MISS BROOKS *moves to* C *stage.*] Elaine—bring me a box of soap flakes—open it.

ELAINE. Yes, Miss Brooks. [*Opens box of soap flakes and crosses to* MISS BROOKS.]

MARTIN. What are you going to do?

MISS BROOKS. Demonstrate. Doris, get a small piece of wood and hold it against the bike spokes. [DORIS *hunts for a piece of wood at* L *stage.*]

STANLEY. You're not going to hurt my bike?

MISS BROOKS. Start pumping. [STANLEY *does.*] Now, Doris—with the stick—just touch them. [DORIS *does as she is instructed. There is a whirring sound.*]

SYLVIA. So?

MISS BROOKS. That isn't a piece of wood and a bicycle wheel—that's the whir of a plane flying toward Shangri-La. [*Gets up on chair at C stage.*] There's a storm raging. You can hear the thunder. [*Shakes tin, and it sounds like thunder.*] The plane is getting closer——Harder, Stanley.

STANLEY [*pumping harder*]. Yes, Miss Brooks.

MARTIN. Here's the spotlight! [*Turns spotlight on* MISS BROOKS.]

MISS BROOKS. The storm is getting worse! [*Starts to shake soap flakes from box with her other hand.*] It's started to snow— the plane may not make it——Stanley, it's getting closer! [STANLEY *pumps still harder.*] The thunder's crashing. [*Shakes tin much harder.*] It's snowing harder—it's a blizzard! [*She is scattering soap flakes on both sides.*]

[MR. WADSWORTH *and* MRS. ALLEN *enter* L *and stop dumbfounded at the sight.* MISS BROOKS *doesn't see them. She continues.*]

MISS BROOKS. The plane reaches the mountains of Shangri-La— the storm is at its height—thunder—more snow! [*She is shaking tin much harder, and scattering soap flakes more rapidly at the same time with other hand.*] It's coming down like—[*Sees them.*]—like—Martin—cut the light. [*Gets down off her chair.*] That's all, Stanley. Thank you.

MRS. ALLEN [*to* MR. WADSWORTH]. Just what I was telling you.

MR. WADSWORTH. What's the meaning of this?

MISS BROOKS. I was demonstrating.

MR. WADSWORTH. I could see that.

MISS BROOKS. I was showing them how we'll work some of the effects for the play.

MRS. ALLEN. There must be a more organized, dignified way of handling such things.

MISS BROOKS. There is—a sound system, mixers, amplifiers, records. But the way I'm doing it—[*At* MR. WADSWORTH.]— it doesn't *cost* anything. [*Then, quickly, to* MRS. ALLEN.] You'll be surprised how well it is going to turn out the night of the production.

MRS. ALLEN. By the night of the production, it's too late to make any changes.

MR. WADSWORTH [*to* MRS. ALLEN]. Perhaps you'd like to wait in my office.

MRS. ALLEN. I'll be glad to. [*Goes out* L.]

MISS BROOKS [*realizing a storm is coming, to* OTHERS]. I think you'd all better go along to the gym. Sylvia can prompt. Try the start of Act Three. [*They start going out* R.]

MR. WADSWORTH. Keeping them till after midnight—I'd expect you to be a little further along.

MARGE [*hesitantly, turning back*]. Mr. Wadsworth—about that midnight——

MISS BROOKS. Never mind, Marge—you scoot along. Try to keep them from annoying the coach. [MARGE *nods and goes out* R, *the last of the students to go out.*]

MR. WADSWORTH [*crossing to* C]. I'm glad you're beginning to give some consideration to our athletic director.

MISS BROOKS [*earnesly*]. Oh, I consider him a lot!

MR. WADSWORTH. Then I wish you'd stop snapping at each other.

MISS BROOKS [*fervently*]. So do I. [*Replaces tin and soap flakes at* L *stage.*]

MR. WADSWORTH [*his voice rising*]. Then why don't you? And why don't you get along better with Miss Audubon? And for heaven's sake, why don't you get along with Mrs. Allen? [MISS BROOKS *shrugs helplessly.* MR. WADSWORTH *continues sharply.*] Well?

MISS BROOKS. Maybe it's because I'm nervous about the play. Saturday night, every folding-chair in the gym's going to be filled with an aunt, uncle, father, mother, cousin, board member, the entire P.T.A.—everyone expecting a Theatre Guild production.

MR. WADSWORTH [*giving a shudder at the thought*]. Saturday! [*Then with his voice quivering with determination and threat.*] It better be good!

MISS BROOKS [*worried*]. I've *got* to have some quiet, uninterrupted rehearsals.

MR. WADSWORTH. You've this room, and the entire east end of the gym. What's stopping you?

MISS BROOKS [*gesturing* L]. Trombones, cornets, tubas—[*Gestures* R.]—and in there—basketball players—[*Demonstrates.*]—dribbling through the stage—shouting and giggling. [*Imitates. In high voice.*] "Don't be nervous—go on and kiss her."

MR. WADSWORTH [*firmly, moving toward her*]. I don't want a lot of kissing.

MISS BROOKS. No, Mr. Wadsworth. [*Crosses and moves* STANLEY'S *bicycle back to* L *stage.*]

MR. WADSWORTH. You may not realize it, but you've other things to take care of—getting the program printed, the set, costumes, make-up, lights!

MISS BROOKS [*gently*]. I realize.

MR. WADSWORTH. It's your responsibility. [*Righteously.*] I can't do everything.

MISS BROOKS [*pleasantly*]. It's a good thing I can.

MR. WADSWORTH [*quickly*]. I don't want you spending a lot of money.

MISS BROOKS. You've mentioned that. [*Pauses behind her desk.*]

MR. WADSWORTH. Last year you came in with a big list of expenses, and most of the ticket money spent. How much has been taken in this year?

MISS BROOKS. Jane's in charge of tickets. The last time she told me, it was about three hundred dollars.

MR. WADSWORTH. Jane Drew? [MISS BROOKS *nods.*] We've had trouble with her. You'd better take charge of those funds. That's a lot of money to leave with a student.

MISS BROOKS. If it wasn't for Jane—and maybe Ted Wilder—nothing would get done. They're a big help.

MR. WADSWORTH. I understand Ted Wilder's marks have fallen off. We don't want this acting to make him ineligible.

MISS BROOKS [*firmly*]. He's carrying quite a load in addition to the play. There's homework, tuning a sports car, some basketball practice, and going steady with two girls.

MR. WADSWORTH. Rhonda Allen and who else?

MISS BROOKS [*wishing she hadn't said so much, reluctantly*]. Jane.

MR. WADSWORTH [*bursting out, pacing to C stage*]. Why does that girl keep cropping up? The "Best Theme" award—the best part in the play—and now this. [*Worried.*] She's infuriating Mrs. Allen's daughter.

MISS BROOKS [*agreeing dolefully*]. Her *only* daughter.

MR. WADSWORTH [*sternly*]. I'm warning you, Brooks. I have to deal with Mrs. Allen day in—day out—on matters that really affect the welfare of this school. [*Determined.*] I'm *not* going to have her antagonized over something completely unimportant!

MISS BROOKS [*equally determined*]. She has no cause for antagonism.

MR. WADSWORTH [*as though not liking the taste of the words*]. As tactfully as I could phrase it, that's what I told her. [MISS BROOKS *is surprised.*] I told her you have my full confidence—that you'd do an *excellent* job with the play. [*Takes a breath, and his voice rises sharply.*] And by heaven——

MISS BROOKS [*swallowing uneasily*]. Yes, Mr. Wadsworth.

MR. WADSWORTH [*his voice still high*]. I don't want any more trouble! Not *any!*

MISS BROOKS [*quickly*]. No, Mr. Wadsworth.

[*The* COACH *enters* R.]

COACH [*crossing to* MR. WADSWORTH]. You wanted to see me?

MR. WADSWORTH. In my office.

COACH [*respectfully*]. Now or later?

MR. WADSWORTH [*unhappily*]. It doesn't matter. I have to find out why the basketball team made such a poor showing Saturday.

MISS BROOKS [*helpfully*]. They won.

MR. WADSWORTH. By two points from a weak opponent. I understand the teamwork was sloppy. I suppose you have an excuse?

[MISS BROOKS *watches* COACH.]

COACH [*shaking his head*]. I'm afraid not. We'll try to do better next game.
MR. WADSWORTH [*irritated*]. I was hoping you'd give me something I could tell people.
COACH. I wish I could.
MISS BROOKS. It's the rehearsals. Ted Wilder doesn't work out with the others, and it interferes with proper practice. [COACH *lets out a slight sigh of relief.*]
MR. WADSWORTH [*to* COACH]. Is that true?
COACH [*speaking carefully*]. Naturally, certain activities take time from other activities.
MR. WADSWORTH. Then Ted Wilder'd better drop the play.
MISS BROOKS [*in agony, crossing to him*]. Mr. Wadsworth—it goes on in a week! I couldn't possibly replace Ted. Someone would have to memorize lines—stage business——Please, Mr. Wadsworth!
COACH [*quickly*]. I can spare Ted till after Saturday. I don't really need him till Monday afternoon. [MISS BROOKS *lets out a short sigh of relief and shoots a look of thanks at* COACH.]
MR. WADSWORTH [*with a dark look at* MISS BROOKS *as he crosses to door* L]. That play's in back of all my trouble.
MISS BROOKS [*after him*]. I'm terribly sorry——[*But* MR. WADSWORTH *has gone out* L. COACH *and* MISS BROOKS *relax.*]
MISS BROOKS [*coming back to* C *stage*]. Thanks, Hugo. If he'd taken Ted it would have wrecked the play.
COACH [*smiling*]. Thanks for getting me off the hook on the game. We didn't do very well.
MISS BROOKS [*contritely*]. And it's *my* fault.
COACH [*calming her*]. I wouldn't really say that.
MISS BROOKS [*sadly*]. The trouble is—it's true.
COACH. Now, now.
MISS BROOKS [*discouraged*]. I don't wonder you've come to hate me. [*Sinks down at one of the students' desks.*]
COACH [*astonished, crossing toward her*]. Hate you! Hey, listen

—just because I blow my top now and then—that doesn't mean I hate you.

MISS BROOKS. You don't?

COACH. Of course not.

MISS BROOKS [*considering this a moment, then with calculation*]. I'm glad, because there's something I wanted to discuss.

COACH [*puzzled*]. With me?

MISS BROOKS [*nodding briefly, then speaking distinctly*]. There were some questions I wanted to ask about your hobby—[*Innocently.*]—about sailing.

COACH [*surprised*]. Sailing?

MISS BROOKS. That *is* your hobby?

COACH. You bet it is. [*Sits on edge of one of the students' desks and faces her.*] But I thought you were only interested in cruise steamers.

MISS BROOKS [*in horror*]. And visit banana ports?

COACH [*hooked*]. You know they mark up prices when cruise ships come in.

MISS BROOKS [*hanging on his words*]. That *very* interesting.

COACH [*seriously*]. It certainly is to a person on a budget.

MISS BROOKS [*quickly*]. I've been on a budget all my life—[*Swallows.*]—and you'd be surprised what an economical shopper I am. [*Warning him.*] A meat market or a grocery store will take advantage of a man every time—[*Meaningfully.*]—but if he has a *woman* to do his shopping——

COACH. I just stay away from the high-priced towns.

MISS BROOKS. Yes, but what do you do around here?

COACH. Eat at the cafeteria.

MISS BROOKS [*severely*]. A person should have home-cooked meals. It's a funny thing, but I'm never too tired to fix a steak—or chops—[*Watches him for a reaction.*]—vegetables—desserts—[*Trying harder.*]—sometimes I bake.

COACH [*obliviously*]. You said you wanted to ask me about sailing.

MISS BROOKS [*rising, moving to* C]. Yes. . . . [*Tries to recall.*]

This sailboat of yours. Is it a—[*Thinks a moment.*]—yawl, ketch, or schooner?

COACH [*immediately interested*]. A sweet little ketch.

MISS BROOKS. Is it gaff rigged or marconi?

COACH. Marconi.

MISS BROOKS. I always liked gaff rig because—[*Hesitates.*]—oh, because the center of effort is lower on the sail.

COACH [*surprised, rising*]. Very few people know that.

MISS BROOKS [*modestly, sitting on chair at* C *stage*]. Naturally anyone who's had a life-long interest in sailing——

COACH [*regarding her thoughtfully*]. A life-long interest. . . . [*Then back to the subject.*] Gaff rig is strong, but when a person sails alone, marconi's easier to handle.

MISS BROOKS. A person may not *always* sail alone.

COACH [*considering it, moving toward her*]. I've been thinking about that. [*Thoughtfully.*] Having someone along to help—it might be all right. If I could just find someone.

MISS BROOKS [*eagerly*]. There's so much someone could do—fix meals—tidy the cabin, take care of shopping. Two can sail as cheaply as one.

COACH [*nodding*]. You're right [*Continues emphatically.*] I ought to hire a cook.

MISS BROOKS. But that would cost so much.

COACH. Maybe I could get one to go along—just for the trip. [*Crosses and sits on students' desk* L C.]

MISS BROOKS. I guess you've never heard of the A F of L and the CIO. What you need is cheap labor. [*Pauses. Then takes the plunge.*] What you need is a wife!

COACH [*shocked*]. Me?

MISS BROOKS [*trying to seem casual*]. That's just the observation of a disinterested observer.

COACH. A wife! [*Jumps up.*] You're crazy!

MISS BROOKS [*stung*]. Mark my words—someday you'll be out in the middle of the Gulf Stream all alone—and you'll start talking to yourself.

COACH [*startled, his hand to his mouth*]. I already talk to myself.

MISS BROOKS [*folding her arms*]. You see?

COACH [*smiling sheepishly*]. Maybe they ought to lock me up.

MISS BROOKS. There's a simpler solution.

COACH [*thinking about it*]. I guess it's important, having help with cooking and shopping—but what a person really needs is someone to see things with, and wonder with—about what might happen tomorrow.

MISS BROOKS [*seriously, thoughtfully*]. It's hard to enjoy things all by yourself—even around here.

COACH. After school, and not counting plays and things— you're by yourself a lot? [MISS BROOKS *nods.*]

MISS BROOKS. You? [COACH *nods.*] Every year I dream about a real vacation, but I always end up as camp counselor. [*Sincerely interested.*] What do you see when you're off sailing?

COACH [*shrugging*]. Nothing special. [*But his interest grows as he talks and moves close to her.*] Porpoises cutting water— jellyfish floating by—maybe a black-footed albatross overhead—seems like they hardly move a wing. The best part is when you're coming up on a strange island. At first it's just a dark outline against the sky, and you wonder what it's going to be like.

MISS BROOKS [*raptly, as though she were looking at the island*]. What's it going to be like?

COACH [*ruefully*]. That's the sort of time I start talking to myself.

MISS BROOKS [*smiling*]. It might get worse. You *should* get married.

COACH [*half joking*]. Where would I find a wife who'd stand school three seasons, and then want to go sailing? [MISS BROOKS *regards her fingernails.* COACH *turns towards her, an idea slowly dawning.*] You know so much about sailing, I bet you've been interested in it for a long, long time.

MISS BROOKS. I can truthfully say that as a child of five or six, one of my favorite toys was a model sailboat.

COACH. Say, Brooks—after rehearsal tonight, I wonder if you'd like to go for a walk, or something. Maybe we could catch a late movie.

MISS BROOKS [*delighted*]. Why, Hugo!

COACH [*so pleased with her*]. Imagine—you were already interested in sailing at the age of five or six! [*Smiles.*] It makes me mad to think of all the time we wasted fighting.

[MISS FINCH *enters* L, *carrying two books.*]

MISS BROOKS. It makes me mad, too. We could have been talking about——

COACH [*enthusiastically*]. Sailing! Navigation! Seamanship! I bet you know more about it than I do.

MISS FINCH [*cheerfully*]. Not yet, but she will. [*To* MISS BROOKS, *coming to* L C.] I found two more books on the subject.

COACH [*puzzled*]. Books? [MISS BROOKS *is waving for silence.*]

MISS FINCH [*reading*]. The "A.B.C's of Sailing," and Mahon's "The Influence of Seapower on History." [*To* MISS BROOKS.] I'm not sure "The Influence of Seapower on History" is the sort of book you had in mind.

MISS BROOKS [*quickly*]. Yes. Thanks a lot.

COACH [*wonderingly*]. The "A.B.C's of Sailing"?

MISS FINCH [*with cheerful agreement*]. Suddenly she's reading up on it. I've been combing the library.

MISS BROOKS [*weakly*]. A sort of refresher course.

MISS FINCH [*surprised*]. Refresher! [*Stops short, however, at sharp look she receives from* MISS BROOKS.]

COACH [*taking one of the books from* MISS FINCH]. The "A—B—C's"? . . .

MISS BROOKS [*taking book from him*]. It's very advanced. [*Tries to pass it off with a smile.*] It really should be titled the "M.O.P.Q's."

COACH [*suddenly recalling*]. Say, I better get on to the gym. [*Starts* R.]

MISS BROOKS [*quickly*]. Hugo—[*Swallows.*]—that's a date for later?

COACH. Sure. [*Shoots another puzzled glance at* MISS FINCH *and then goes out* R.]

MISS FINCH. Did I say something wrong?

MISS BROOKS [*woefully*]. I don't know—[*Looks after* COACH.] —yet.

MISS FINCH. I thought he was interested in sailing.

MISS BROOKS. He is. [*Still looking after him, she nods.*] Every summer he goes to Martinique and the Grenadines. [*Back to* MISS FINCH.] He's not just a muscle-man. He's sensitive and understanding and observes things.

MISS FINCH [*practically*]. What things?

MISS BROOKS [*looking after him again*]. Things like porpoises and albatrosses and jellyfish. [*To* MISS FINCH, *explaining.*] They float by. [*Makes floating gesture with hand.*]

MISS FINCH [*unimpressed*]. You want to see jellyfish?

MISS BROOKS [*thinking about it*]. Imagine—working at the same school with your husband, and then sailing off every summer—you come up on a strange island, and then you wonder what it's going to be like.

MISS FINCH. Then you find out what it's like—sand flies, no sanitation, a sunbaked misery.

MISS BROOKS. That doesn't scare a summer camp counselor with six years' seniority. [*Takes other book from* MISS FINCH, *crosses to her desk, and puts books in drawer.*]

MISS FINCH. Does Mrs. Allen scare you? If she was after my scalp, she'd scare me.

MISS BROOKS. More fuss with the school board?

MISS FINCH. You'd better thank heaven the rest of the board members are all so swell. I'd try hard to keep things extra smooth and quiet right now.

MISS BROOKS [*earnestly*]. I'm trying.

[DORIS *enters* R.]

DORIS [*coming to* C]. Miss Brooks—they're passing basketballs back and forth across the stage.

MISS BROOKS. Tell them to get out of the east end of the gym—politely.

DORIS. I *already* told them.

[JANE *enters* R.]

JANE [*coming to* C]. It's all right. Ted made them move off.

MISS BROOKS [*to* DORIS]. Tell the others I'll be right in. [DORIS *nods and goes out* R. MISS FINCH *moves* L.]

MISS FINCH. I'd better get back upstairs. The trombones'll be starting.

MISS BROOKS. They usually hold off till I begin rehearsal.

MISS FINCH [*as she goes*]. Just remember—smooth and quiet. [*Goes out* L. JANE *has been watching this. She comes toward* L C.]

JANE. Is anything *wrong* with rehearsal?

MISS BROOKS [*nodding*]. Simultaneous music and basketball practice.

JANE [*anxiously*]. We shouldn't let *anything* interfere. It's such a wonderful play.

MISS BROOKS [*sitting at her desk*]. With all the ruckus, how can you tell?

JANE. I can tell.

MISS BROOKS [*looking closely at her*]. Would it still be wonderful, if Ted wasn't in it?

JANE [*after a pause*]. No.

MISS BROOKS. I see.

JANE. Do you?

MISS BROOKS [*after a moment, nodding*]. I do.

JANE. The play's the only chance I have. Afterwards, he'll be back at basketball—then baseball——

MISS BROOKS [*smiling*]. And you'll be back in the grandstand.

JANE [*nodding*]. He'll notice me as much as one of the wooden benches. [*Concerned.*] Maybe if the play's a big success—maybe he'll remember a little—later on.

MISS BROOKS [*repressing a smile*]. I hear you were a bit lavish with the Swiss steaks.

JANE. Do you know if *he* knows? [MISS BROOKS *shakes her head.*] I'm going to tell him I came into some money—or something—so I quit. I don't want him feeling sorry for me. Maybe I could let him see some of the ticket money—sort of accidentally.

MISS BROOKS [*remembering*]. Say, Jane—Mr. Wadsworth thought I'd better take personal charge of those funds.

JANE [*coming in front of* MISS BROOKS' *desk*]. It'll be a relief. I have a record of how many tickets to everyone, and what they've turned in. I don't know if it's home, or in my locker.

MISS BROOKS. Better get it to me tomorrow. Mr. Wadsworth suggested it—and he's a little excitable these days.

JANE [*smiling*]. You should have heard him go on at me. I thought I was going to be expelled.

MISS BROOKS. Don't worry about that job. I think I can find you some baby-sitting.

JANE [*delightedly*]. Gosh, could you?

MISS BROOKS. It doesn't pay much, but then you want to be an English teacher. [*With smile.*] You might as well get used to poverty.

JANE [*concerned*]. We'd better get on with rehearsal.

MISS BROOKS [*glancing* L]. Still no French horns. [*Wistfully.*] If we could only have one quiet, uninterrupted rehearsal—just one!

JANE. Just one?

MISS BROOKS [*nodding*]. At least then I could get a perspective on the play as a whole.

JANE [*anxiously*]. Couldn't we do something?

MISS BROOKS. I don't know what.

[TED *enters* R.]

TED [*coming to* C]. All set to try the snow effect past the window.

MISS BROOKS. Good.

TED. I had to chase the basketballers again. They're just fooling around. The coach didn't call a regular practice for today.

JANE [*crossing to him*]. If it isn't a regular practice—why let them mess around?

TED. What can you do?

JANE. Take the basketballs. Lock them in Miss Brooks' office.

TED. You're crazy!

JANE. You said it wasn't a regular practice. If you took the basketballs——

TED [*to* MISS BROOKS]. What do *you* think?

MISS BROOKS. Of course, I'd be glad for a quiet rehearsal.

JANE [*imperatively*]. We've *got* to get a perspective.

TED. You want me to grab all the basketballs?

JANE [*pushing him toward* R]. Yes. Go get them!

TED. I don't know about this. . . . [*Goes out* R.]

JANE [*defensively, to* MISS BROOKS]. He said it wasn't a regular practice. [*Nervously, crossing toward* MISS BROOKS.] If they don't have basketballs, they can't keep interrupting, can they?

MISS BROOKS. I guess not.

JANE [*worried*]. You said you *need* a perspective, didn't you?

MISS BROOKS. Yes.

JANE. The time's so short. We ought to have that rehearsal today.

MISS BROOKS. We certainly should. It's just that I get nervous.

JANE. So do I.

[TED *enters* R, *carrying all the basketballs he can hold.*]

TED [*coming to* R C]. Nothing to it. I just said I needed them.

JANE [*unhappily, crossing* U R C]. Wonderful! [*Opens door* U R C.] Better put them in here. [TED *starts* U R C.]

MISS BROOKS [*rising, crossing after him*]. Be careful of those Chinese vases. [TED *goes out* U R C.]

TED [*calling back*]. The what?

MISS BROOKS. Chinese vases. [*There is a crash of glass breaking, off* U R C.]

JANE [*horrified*]. No! [*Turns away, afraid to look.*]

MISS BROOKS [*wincing, likewise turning away*]. Oh, no! Oh, no!

[TED *re-enters* U R C, *looking very apologetic.*]

TED. I'm awfully sorry.

MISS BROOKS [*reproachfully*]. Ted . . .

TED [*apologetically*]. The mason jar with the paper clips and rubber bands—I didn't see it at all.

MISS BROOKS. The mason jar? [TED *nods, and both she and* JANE *heave a sigh of relief, and relax.*]

TED. Do you want me to pick up now?

MISS BROOKS [*weakly*]. No. [*Shakes her head.*] We'd better take advantage of the momentary lull in the gym.

JANE [*determined*]. The play could still be interrupted. [*Starts* L.] I'll be right back. [*Goes out* L.]

TED. Now what?

MISS BROOKS [*shaking her head; she doesn't know*]. Maybe she's going to lock up Mr. Wadsworth. [*Crosses to* L C.]

TED [*coming to* C]. For a meek sort of character, she seems to get fairly determined.

MISS BROOKS. I'm surprised you noticed.

TED. I seem to be getting very democratic.

MISS BROOKS. Isn't Rhonda Allen more your type?

TED. She's a girl.

MISS BROOKS. I understand Jane gave you real value today on the thirty-one cent luncheon.

TED [*nodding*]. I happened to mention I was hungry. [*Concerned.*] If she doesn't watch out she'll get in trouble, dishing up portions like that.

MISS BROOKS [*dryly*]. It wouldn't surprise me a bit.

[JANE *comes in* L, *carrying as many band instruments as she can handle or are available.*]

TED [*as he sees her*]. Holy cow!

MISS BROOKS [*stunned*]. Jane!

JANE [*anxiously*]. I don't think anyone saw me. [*Indicates door* U R C.] Open the door—quick. [TED *hurries* U R C *and opens door as* JANE *staggers* U R C. *She speaks in a worried voice, over her shoulder, to* MISS BROOKS.] Now we'll have a real rehearsal. [*Goes out* U R C *with instruments.*]

TED [*to* MISS BROOKS, *with a gesture, mockingly*]. The show must go on.

MISS BROOKS [*worried*]. Oh, my heaven! . . .

TED [*indicating her office*]. It'll be getting a little crowded in there. What are you going to do?

MISS BROOKS. What *can* I do?

[JANE *re-enters* U R C.]

MISS BROOKS. Oh, Jane . . .

JANE [*quickly, coming to* C]. It's all my idea, and I'll take the blame.

MISS BROOKS. You're in no position to take on any more blame.

JANE. Gosh, Miss Brooks, we'd better get started.

MISS BROOKS. We'll have it right here. I'll round them up. [*Starts* R.]

TED [*crossing to* L *stage, picking up two boxes of soap flakes*]. Don't you want to try out the snow effect past the window?

MISS BROOKS. I can try it myself. [*Indicates* JANE.] Better keep an eye on her. [TED *crosses and hands soap flakes to* MISS BROOKS.]

JANE [*with a quaver, to* MISS BROOKS]. Are you mad?

MISS BROOKS. Of course not. [*Goes out* R.]

TED [*crossing to* JANE]. Say—I want to thank you for all the Swiss steaks.

JANE. You're welcome.

TED. Tomorrow—I'll only want two.

JANE. I can't help tomorrow—I—I quit the job. [*Turns and sits at students' desk* L C.]

TED. Quit your job!

JANE. You see—I came into a good bit of money. [*Swallows.*] I don't need to bother with that job any more.

TED [*sitting astride chair at* C *stage*]. Swell!

JANE. Of course, I'm so used to working—I might take up some other sort of job. I thought it might be very interesting to do a little baby-sitting—because it's so interesting.

TED. It is?

JANE. Some of those places don't mind if you help yourself to the refrigerator.

TED. What's that got to do with me?

JANE [*trying still harder*]. Some of those places don't mind if boys sit with girls who sit with babies.

TED [*thoughtlessly*]. Anytime I want a really full refrigerator, I drop in on ...

JANE [*defeated*]. I know.

TED. Is anything wrong?

JANE [*swallowing, nodding*]. Everything.

TED. I thought you just came into a lot of money.

JANE [*depreciatingly*]. That ...

TED [*trying to cheer her*]. You're doing swell in the part of Helen.

JANE [*delighted*]. You think so?

TED [*rising*]. You really put feeling in it. I mean, if I were actually Conway, and you were actually Helen, and if we were actually at Shangri-La, and you didn't want me to leave —[*Takes a breath.*]—I wouldn't.

JANE [*deeply pleased*]. You'd stay?

TED [*crossing toward her*]. If you asked me—like you ask me in the play.

JANE. You mean: [*Quotes, speaking with feeling, as she rises.*] "Don't go."

TED [*nods*]. Then you ... [*Raises fingers to his lips.*]

JANE. I know.

TED. Don't you think we ought to rehearse?

JANE. I guess I already know that part.

TED. You're sure?

JANE [*looking at him, nodding slowly, then:*]. "You belong here, Conway. And—I want you to stay. Don't go." [*Slowly starts to bring her face up to kiss him.*]

[*Before* JANE *can kiss him, the door* R *bursts open.* ELSIE *enters, followed by* FAITH *and* ELAINE. *They carry playbooks.* JANE *stops where she is, but continues to look at* TED.]

ELSIE [*coming to* C *with* ELAINE]. Rehearsal, calling rehearsal.
ELAINE. We should use the gym.
FAITH. Miss Brooks says here. [*Neither* TED *nor* JANE *has looked away from the other.*]
TED [*to* JANE]. It's really a swell play.
JANE. "Lost Horizon." I'll never forget. [*Swallows.*] Some things a person just wouldn't ever forget.

[RHONDA *enters* R.]

ELSIE [*at sight of* TED *and* JANE]. Mah goodness!
RHONDA. What's going on? [*Comes to* C.]
TED. Rehearsal.
TED. Isn't it enough?
FAITH [*disappointed*]. Is that all?
JANE [*suddenly deciding, to* TED]. No! No, it isn't!

[*The surprise at this is cut by the entrance of* MARGE, DORIS, *and* SYLVIA. *They join the other girls at* C *stage.*]

MARGE. Miss Brooks says get ready.
SYLVIA. Clear off the middle space.
DORIS. She's going to take it right through from the beginning.
ELAINE [*alarmed*]. That means my part and Faith's part right away.
FAITH [*opening her playbook rapidly*]. Oh, dear! [FAITH *and* ELAINE *start lip-reading their parts.* DORIS *starts setting up some chairs to indicate entrances.*]
RHONDA [*crossing to* JANE]. What do you mean, a rehearsal isn't enough.
JANE [*hesitantly, embarrassed*]. I meant——
TED [*cutting in*]. Forget it. Let's get going.
RHONDA [*to* JANE]. I asked you a question.

MARGE [*to* RHONDA, *as she arranges chair in a specific spot at* C *stage*]. Hey—how about doing a little work?
SYLVIA. Join the common people.
ELSIE. It's so nice and quiet today. We ought to start rehearsal.
TED [*apprehensively*]. In a hurry.

[MISS AUDUBON *bursts in* L.]

MISS AUDUBON. Quiet! All of you—quiet. [ALL *instantly stop what they are doing, and look at her.*] Where is she? I know she's responsible. Where is she?
TED. Miss Brooks?
MISS AUDUBON. You know very well. [*Turns.*] I'm going to get Mr. Wadsworth. [*Goes out* L.]
MARGE. What got into her?
ELAINE. Who knows.
RHONDA. Maybe there's a reason.

[STANLEY *enters* R.]

STANLEY [*joining others*]. Wow—you should see the way the fan's blowing soapflakes!
MARGE. Like a blizzard in Tibet?
STANLEY [*enthusiastically*]. They're all over the gym.
DORIS [*glumly*]. Probably I'll have to sweep up.

[MISS BROOKS *enters* R.]

ELSIE. Wouldn't hurt you.
RHONDA [*shrugging*]. Leave it for the janitor—or Miss Brooks.
MISS BROOKS [*coming to* C]. The janitor and Miss Brooks have enough to do. I want all of you who aren't in the first scene to step over here. [*Indicates* L *stage.*] Faith, you can use that chair, and we'll pretend there's a table in front of you. [FAITH *sits at chair at* C *stage. The* OTHERS *sit or stand at* L *stage.*]
MARGE. Miss Brooks.
MISS BROOKS. Yes.
MARGE. Miss Audubon was just looking for you.
SYLVIA. She seemed very upset.

Act II   Our Miss Brooks   Page 71

DORIS. Said she was going to get Mr. Wadsworth.

MISS BROOKS [*looking at* JANE, *who nods mournfully, then sighing*]. I guess we might as well start, anyway—while we can. Now, Faith—

[*The* COACH *enters* R.]

COACH [*coming to* R C]. Miss Brooks.

MISS BROOKS [*turning*]. Yes—[*With touch of warmth.*]—Hugo.

COACH [*smiling*]. That soap has the gym floor about ready for another dance.

MISS BROOKS. I'm terribly sorry. You see——

COACH. That's all right. I wanted to ask you about something else entirely. I know it's silly even to ask, but——

MISS BROOKS [*cutting in*]. I understand you have no regular basketball practice today.

COACH [*smiling*]. After the remarks, I called a special session. I just happened to wonder if you happened to know—where——

[*The door* L *bursts open and* MISS AUDUBON *enters, followed by* MR. WADSWORTH *and* MRS. ALLEN.]

MR. WADSWORTH [*as he enters*]. I can't believe it.

MISS AUDUBON. You'll see. [*Follows* MR. WADSWORTH *to* C.]

MRS. ALLEN [*following to* C *stage*]. It wouldn't surprise me a bit.

MR. WADSWORTH. Miss Brooks, I feel foolish, asking you this, but do you know where any of the band instruments are?

COACH. That's funny. I was just going to ask her if she knew the whereabouts of my basketballs.

MRS. ALLEN. The basketballs, too!

MR. WADSWORTH [*to* MISS BROOKS]. I'm asking you a direct question. Do you have any idea where the band instruments and basketballs are?

JANE [*stepping forward*]. Mr. Wadsworth——

MR. WADSWORTH. I'm speaking to Miss Brooks.

MISS BROOKS [*nodding resignedly*]. They're in my office.
MISS AUDUBON [*triumphantly*]. You see!
MR. WADSWORTH. Your office?
COACH [*dumbfounded*]. The basketballs, too? [MISS BROOKS *nods miserably.*]
JANE. It was my idea. I did it.
MR. WADSWORTH [*to* MISS BROOKS]. Will you get them at once?
JANE [*hurriedly*]. I will. [*Hurries out* U R C.]
MRS. ALLEN. We'll discuss this at the next board meeting.
MR. WADSWORTH. I agree.

[*There is a loud crash from off* U R C. ALL *freeze. Then* JANE *comes in* U R C *with her arms full of band instruments, and her eyes shut with pain.*]

MISS AUDUBON [*at sight of instruments*]. There they are!
JANE [*takes a sudden breath, and swallowing a sob*]. I broke it.
MR. WADSWORTH. Broke what?
JANE. One of the Chinese vases.
MRS. ALLEN. *My* Chinese vase!
MISS BROOKS. Oh, Jane, dear!
JANE [*ready to be burned at the stake*]. Do whatever you want to me. [*Staggers to* C *with instruments.*]
MISS BROOKS [*unhappily*]. I'd better get the basketballs. [*Hurries out* U R C.]
MRS. ALLEN. That was a valuable vase. I warned her, too. I warned her especially.
TED. Accidents happen.
RHONDA. Accidentally on purpose.

[MISS BROOKS *enters* U R C, *turning sideways to get through the door with the basketballs.*]

MISS BROOKS. Here you are. [*But a basketball falls from her arms back into office.* NOTE: *It can be pushed from underneath by her hand. Her head bobs twice as she follows the bounce. Then she shuts her eyes. There is another loud crash off* U R C.]

MRS. ALLEN [*rushing to door* U R C]. The other one—she did it on purpose! You all saw her.

RHONDA. And so did Jane.

MRS. ALLEN. My valuable vases! [*Comes back to* C.] They're worth several hundred dollars! [*To* MR. WADSWORTH.] What are you going to do about it? [MISS BROOKS *moves helplessly to* C, *her arms full of basketballs.*]

MISS AUDUBON [*as she takes instruments from* JANE]. What are you going to do about her hiding the band instruments?

MRS. ALLEN. Not to mention the basketballs.

MR. WADSWORTH. All of you young people—go on to the gym—snap along. Along now. [ALL *the students except* JANE, TED, *and* RHONDA *go out* R.]

COACH [*puzzled, to* MISS BROOKS]. I can't understand why you'd do a thing like this—after the way we talked.

JANE. It was I. It wasn't Miss Brooks.

MRS. ALLEN. She knew all about it.

MISS BROOKS [*nodding*]. I did. We wanted to have one peaceful, quiet, uninterrupted rehearsal.

MRS. ALLEN. You'd think the play was the only thing that matters.

JANE. We just wanted one rehearsal—and it *does* matter.

MISS BROOKS. Hush, dear.

MR. WADSWORTH [*severely*]. Have you taken over the ticket money from this girl?

MISS BROOKS. Not yet.

MR. WADSWORTH [*his voice rising*]. I specifically told you——

JANE. I didn't have it.

MR. WADSWORTH. Didn't have it!

JANE. I mean, I'm not sure where I left it—exactly.

MR. WADSWORTH [*bursting*]. Not sure—not sure about three hundred dollars!

TED. Holy cow, Jane—is that the money you suddenly came into?

JANE. Yes—I mean, no.

TED [*shaking his head*]. My gosh—the ticket money. . . .

JANE. I didn't do anything with it.

MISS BROOKS. Of course not.

MR WADSWORTH [*bitterly, to* MISS BROOKS]. You've got the money misplaced—broken expensive vases—rehearsals after midnight—hidden band instruments—interferred with basketball practice——

[STANLEY *rushes in* R.]

STANLEY [*coming to* R C]. Miss Brooks—all the soap flakes you scattered on the floor—Martin just slipped and fell. I think he sprained something.

MR. WADSWORTH [*verging on explosion*]. Soap—*you* scattered! *Now* someone's hurt! [*Burning.*] Ohh! . . . [*Hurries out* R, *followed by* STANLEY.]

MRS. ALLEN. The board's going to hear it all. [*To* RHONDA.] Come along. [*Goes out* R.]

RHONDA [*to* TED]. Coming?

TED. Right with you. [RHONDA *goes out* R. MISS AUDUBON, *her arms full of musical instruments, starts* L *with them.*]

MISS AUDUBON. Hah! [*Goes out* L.]

TED [*to* JANE]. I thought it was foolish to get the basketballs and band instruments, but playing around with school funds!

JANE [*holding back tears*]. I didn't, Ted—I didn't.

MISS BROOKS. You just don't understand.

COACH. I guess I don't understand, either. Tell me one thing—honestly. Did you really have a life-long interest in sailing, or did you just read up on it? Just now?

MISS BROOKS [*unhappily*]. I just read up—but, Hugo——

COACH [*to* TED]. I guess we might as well get along. I'll have to look at Martin's sprain. [TED *nods, as* COACH *starts* R.]

JANE [*as they start, the lines from the play*]. Conway—Ted—*don't go!*

TED [*looking at her a moment, then dismissing her*]. Be seeing you around. [*Goes out* R *with* COACH. *There is a pause.*]

MISS BROOKS [*to* JANE, *her arms still full of basketballs*]. Are you sure you still want to be an English teacher?

JANE [*miserably*]. Since I'll never have a husband or anything—what else is there for an old maid?

MISS BROOKS [*wistfully*]. I wish I knew.

[*The curtain starts down. There is a sudden thud and muffled shouting from off* R. *The door* R *bursts open, and* STANLEY *re-enters.*]

STANLEY [*coming to* R C]. Mr. Wadsworth—he skidded and crashed onto the floor! [*Winces.*] Oh, boy! Like a ton of bricks! [STANLEY *dashes out* R *again.* MISS BROOKS *lets basketballs cascade from her arms to floor, and she and* JANE *put their arms around each other in mutual misery.*]

THE CURTAIN IS DOWN

ACT THREE

AT RISE OF CURTAIN: *The scene is the same. The various properties that have been assembled for the production of "Lost Horizon" have been removed. The time is about eight o'clock, the evening of the play. On the blackboard are several chalked signs such as "All Cast Members Report at 7 P.M. SHARP!" and "No Smoking!"* ELSIE, FAITH, ELAINE, *and* DORIS *are on-stage.* ELSIE *is seated in a chair* D R, *studying her playbook intently. Every now and then she looks off and repeats some line with her lips.* ELAINE *and* FAITH, *wearing evening gowns, are by* MISS BROOKS' *desk, upon which a large mirror is propped.* FAITH *is watching* ELAINE *powder her face.* DORIS, *wearing a dark Chinese-pajama outfit, is peering at herself in a small mirror, propped upon one of the students' desks. She stretches her eyes till they thin.*]

DORIS. Faith—do I look like a Tibetan serving-girl? [FAITH *shakes her head, as* DORIS *stretches her eyes till they are thin slits.*] Now?
FAITH [*nodding*]. Yes—now. [*In afterthought.*] It's terrifying.
ELSIE [*suddenly slamming down her book, in horror*]. I can't remember a line! I've forgotten my lines!
ELAINE. They'll come to you.
ELSIE [*anxiously*]. What if they don't? What'll I do then?
FAITH. You'll just stand there—like a big dummy.
ELSIE [*pointing* R]. My mother and father are coming—also two aunts and Uncle William.

[SYLVIA *enters* R. *She has a clip board in her hand.*]

SYLVIA [*coming to* R C]. Curtain time in thirty minutes—thirty-minute call.
DORIS. Thirty minutes!

ELSIE [*in misery*]. I've forgotten my part! Better tell Miss Brooks.

SYLVIA. You'll remember when the play starts. Don't go bothering Miss Brooks.

[MARGE *enters* L.]

ELAINE. She shouldn't have had dress rehearsal this afternoon. Everyone knows you're supposed to have it the day before.

MARGE [*sarcastically, moving to* C]. I wonder why *Miss Brooks* didn't know?

SYLVIA [*reprimandingly*]. We couldn't get everything assembled till this afternoon.

FAITH. It seems to me Miss Brooks went to a lot of unnecessary worry. [*Gestures blithely.*] Everything got done. Everything got tended to.

MARGE [*nodding*]. A little troop of Brownies came in last night. Miss Brooks and a few of us stayed up to watch them work.

ELSIE. She really looked tired in class today.

DORIS. Say, Marge—[*Pulls her eyes out thin.*]—do I look Tibetan?

MARGE. Let me try with an eyebrow pencil. [*Takes one from* MISS BROOKS' *desk, and as the dialogue proceeds she extends* DORIS' *eye-line.*]

ELSIE. Sylvia—you be ready with that prompt book.

SYLVIA. Just concentrate on the first line. You did swell in rehearsal.

FAITH. That was some audience this afternoon.

ELAINE [*with mock shudder*]. The school board!

DORIS. They made me nervous.

ELSIE [*bothered*]. They didn't say anything. When it was over they just walked out.

MARGE. Rhonda told me they went to a special meeting.

[STANLEY *and* MARTIN *enter* R *and come to* C.]

STANLEY. We looked under the curtain. The gym's half full already.

MARTIN. Everybody's read the book. They want to see the play. [*Sits at students' desk* L C.] Boy, I have to sit down.

DORIS. Nervous?

MARTIN. I've got a pain in my side.

ELSIE [*to* MARTIN]. Have you forgotten any lines?

MARTIN [*wondering*]. Let me think. [*Sits straight up.*] Oh, gosh!

SYLVIA. Don't think. Just relax.

MARTIN. I can't. [*Hand to side.*] I get pains.

ELSIE. If you forgot your lines—what would you do?

MARTIN [*taking papers from his pocket*]. I'll have these notes where the audience can't see.

MARGE. Now I know how you passed history.

MARTIN [*smiling*]. Take it easy. I don't feel so good.

ELSIE [*a new idea*]. Notes! [*Takes out a pencil and a piece of paper, and through the following dialogue makes notes.*]

DORIS [*to* SYLVIA]. How much longer?

SYLVIA [*glancing at watch*]. Twenty-seven minutes. [*A wave of tenseness passes through them all.*]

STANLEY [*has started to say something but can't, then suddenly exclaiming in a hoarse whisper*]. It's gone! [*Comes downstage.*] It's gone!

ELSIE. What?

STANLEY [*in loud whisper*]. My voice! I've lost my voice! [MARTIN *rises and whacks him on seat.* STANLEY *exclaims in a loud and natural tone.*] Ouch! [*Relaxes, sighs with relief, and speaks gratefully to* MARTIN.] Gosh, thanks!

MARTIN. Any time. [*Sits again.*]

STANLEY [*swallowing nervously*]. I thought the dress rehearsal was pretty good. [*Hoping for agreement.*] Didn't the rest of you think it was pretty good?

FAITH [*shrugging*]. How can you tell?

ELAINE. Nobody knows.

MARTIN. All I know is, right afterwards I started getting cramps. [*Holds side.*]

SYLVIA [*encouragingly*]. It was fine! Stop fretting!

MARGE. I know one scene that was *really* something——
DORIS. Ted and Jane? [MARGE *nods.*]
ELAINE. Were they supposed to be acting, or what?
FAITH. Looked to me like she meant it.
DORIS. Just watching them—it made me embarrassed.

[RHONDA *enters* L, *wearing her Chinese costume.*]

FAITH. Offstage they don't even speak to each other.
ELSIE. But on-stage!
RHONDA. What about it? [*Strolls to* C.]
DORIS. Wow!
MARGE [*repressing a smile*]. A realistic performance.
RHONDA. It doesn't mean a thing.
MARGE [*needling*]. Very convincing.
RHONDA [*irritated*]. Just play-acting.
DORIS [*disappointed*]. Is it?
RHONDA [*unable completely to repress her bitterness*]. A person shouldn't be allowed to take advantage of a part in a play. [*Knowingly.*] It wouldn't surprise me if Miss Audubon directs the play after this.
MARGE. You have a hot tip from the board meeting?
SYLVIA. I suppose Miss Brooks doesn't work hard enough?
RHONDA. I just said it wouldn't surprise me.

[MISS BROOKS *enters* R. *She is in a rush. She turns back and calls out the door* R.]

MISS BROOKS. That's fine—just leave the spare fuses there by the box. [*Comes to* C.] How are you all feeling? [*Pauses.*] Terrible? [*There is a general nod, and murmur of agreement.*]
MARTIN. I've got a pain.
MISS BROOKS [*smiling*]. So have I. Doris, when you carry cups that are supposed to be full of tea—remember, they'd weigh something. You'd carry them carefully, so the tea wouldn't spill. Rhonda, don't cross in front of Marge while she's speaking. And, Marge, when someone talks to you on-stage, listen

to them. An actor doesn't speak in turn. He speaks *in response*. [*Notices* ELSIE'S *notes, crosses down to her.*] What's this?

ELSIE. My lines——

MISS BROOKS [*taking notes*]. You know them.

ELSIE [*in horror, as* MISS BROOKS *crumples her notes in a ball*]. Miss Brooks!

[MISS FINCH *enters* L.]

SYLVIA [*reassuring* ELSIE]. I'll have the prompt book ready—in case.

MISS BROOKS [*to* SYLVIA]. Don't be *too* quick with your prompting. Allow time for natural pauses.

MISS FINCH [*coming to* MISS BROOKS]. Elaine's father said he was setting up the cast to all the Cokes they want—if it won't be a disruption. [*There is a reaction of pleasure from the* CAST.] They brought in a tub of ice. It's out of the way—in the music room.

MISS BROOKS. Miss Audubon didn't mind?

MISS FINCH. I guess not.

MISS BROOKS. Any of you want a Coke? . . . [ALL *rise, or step forward.*] Go ahead. [*To* SYLVIA.] You keep track of the time. [*To* ALL.] Relax for a few minutes, and don't talk about the play. [ALL *the* STUDENTS *start out* L.]

MARTIN. Maybe that's what I need.

STANLEY. Me, too—for my voice. [*He and* MARTIN *go out* L.]

DORIS. So long as it's free.

FAITH [*to* ELAINE]. Nice of your father.

MARGE. I should say.

ELAINE [*as she exits*]. He's more excited about the play than I am.

SYLVIA [*hesitating, to* MISS BROOKS]. Anything more I can do?

MISS BROOKS [*smiling*]. See that none of them go wandering off. You've been a wonderful help, Sylvia.

SYLVIA [*embarrassed*]. Gosh, Miss Brooks——[*Then checks her watch.*] Twenty-two more minutes—I'll keep track. [*She is the last to go out* L, *leaving* MISS BROOKS *and* MISS FINCH *alone.*]

MISS FINCH [*worried*]. How was dress rehearsal?

MISS BROOKS. I can't tell. [*Sits at her desk, wearily.*] I'm too close to it. [*Wryly.*] Have they issued a communiqué yet?

MISS FINCH. The school board?

MISS BROOKS. I should have walked in on that meeting and told them I quit.

MISS FINCH [*surprised, crossing toward her, speaking gently*]. Why, Brooks—you really care.

MISS BROOKS [*swallowing*]. Of course I care.

MISS FINCH [*thoughtfully*]. Do you see anything of the coach these days?

MISS BROOKS [*nodding*]. Sometimes we pass in the hall. [*Unhappily.*] He's—polite.

MISS FINCH [*changing subject*]. I guess the board meeting broke up hours ago.

MISS BROOKS. If they decided something about me—[*Bothered.*] —I wish they'd let me know.

MISS FINCH [*smiling*]. If they did, they will.

MISS BROOKS [*smiling wryly*]. I can count on that.

[JANE *enters* U R C. *She is wearing a simple dress for the play, and, if desired, her hair may be up. She is carrying one of* MRS. ALLEN'S *vases. She comes to* C.]

MISS FINCH [*seeing her*]. Where'd you get that vase? [*Rhymes with "case."*]

MISS BROOKS. Hello, Jane. [*Rises.*]

JANE [*smiling*]. It's a vase. [*Broad "a."*] Mrs. Allen's. I glued it. I glued the other one, too.

MISS BROOKS [*examining it*]. Glued it?

JANE [*worried*]. When you look close you can see the cracks.

MISS BROOKS [*smiling*]. That just makes it more antique.

MISS FINCH. My advice is—unglue it.

[MISS AUDUBON *hurries in* L.]

JANE [*shocked*]. Unglue it? [MISS FINCH *nods.*]

MISS AUDUBON [*crossing to* MISS BROOKS]. Miss Brooks! Miss Brooks——

MISS BROOKS [*anxiously*]. They aren't making a mess in the music room?

MISS AUDUBON [*brushing past this*]. A big mess. I wanted to see you about——

MISS BROOKS. I'll straighten it up after the play.

MISS AUDUBON. No, no! I wanted to tell you about the dress rehearsal.

MISS BROOKS. The play?

MISS AUDUBON [*nodding, then sniffing*]. It was beautiful—absolutely beautiful!

MISS BROOKS [*surprised*]. You liked it?

MISS AUDUBON. I could hardly believe it was just Jane and Ted and Marge and Elsie and Doris up there. I'm glad you took over. I'd have never been able to handle it.

MISS BROOKS. Of course you would. Everything's worked out in the playbook. It's a wonderful story.

MISS AUDUBON. Because it has a real meaning. I haven't been so moved since the first time I heard Brahms' "Fourth."

MISS BROOKS [*a little moved herself*]. That's awfully kind.

MISS AUDUBON. I'd like to make it clear that I disassociate myself entirely with any action the school board takes.

MISS BROOKS [*swallowing*]. Action——

MISS AUDUBON. I'd better see to the band. Almost time for our piece. [*Hurries out* R.]

MISS FINCH. The play must really have something. There's been a big run on the original book in the library. [*Turns.*] I'd better get back out front. [*Starts* R.]

JANE. Miss Finch—why did you advise me to *unglue* the vase?

MISS FINCH [*pausing*]. Because Mrs. Allen already collected from the insurance company. [*To* MISS BROOKS.] If it's any help, I disassociate myself, too. [*Goes out* R. JANE *and* MISS BROOKS *are both upset.*]

JANE [*unhappily*]. I did the wrong thing when I broke it. Then

I did the wrong thing when I glued it back together. [*Sits at one of students' desks.*]

MISS BROOKS. I know, dear. That's the story of my life. [*Regards* JANE.] Do you see anything of Ted—offstage?

JANE. Sometimes we pass in the hall. [*With difficulty.*] He's sort of——

MISS BROOKS. Polite? [JANE *nods.* MISS BROOKS *sighs, then:*] Anyway, you catch up with him on-stage.

JANE. Tonight's the last time. When the curtain comes down, it's—[*Swallows.*]—all over.

MISS BROOKS [*moving closer to her*]. Still, you'll be seeing him around.

JANE. From the grandstand. He'll be pretty busy. [*Defends him.*] He has lots of activities. Baseball—[*Bitterly.*]—driving that English hot rod. [*Unhappily.*] And no more play rehearsals to make up for it.

MISS BROOKS. I'm sorry.

JANE. Just the same—[*With feeling.*]—I'm glad about the play, and I'll never forget.

MISS BROOKS [*with a smile*]. You put a lot into your part.

JANE. When it comes to the place tonight—where I'm supposed to—you know—kiss him? It isn't going to be Conway and Helen. It'll be Ted and me—and—[*With difficulty.*]—it'll be like I was kissing him good-bye.

MISS BROOKS [*concerned*]. Jane—maybe he doesn't really know how you feel. Maybe if he knew——

JANE [*seriously*]. Oh, he will! When we get to that part in the play—he will.

MISS BROOKS [*humorously*]. Too bad the coach and I don't have some part in the play.

JANE [*agreeing completely*]. Isn't it?

MISS BROOKS [*taking the idea seriously herself*]. Yes—I guess it is.

[TED *and* COACH *enter* R.]

TED [*as he enters, to* COACH]. Never have crowds like that for basketball. [*Comes to* C *with* COACH.]

COACH. Maybe if they all knew how comical a basketball team can get——[*To* MISS BROOKS *and* JANE.] Hello. [MISS BROOKS *and* JANE *nod in reply.*]

TED [*moving toward* JANE]. Time's getting short.

JANE. Yes.

TED. I'm not nervous. It'll be all over before you know it.

JANE [*swallowing*]. Yes.

COACH [*to* MISS BROOKS]. I loaned Ted my pipe—for the part. [TED *puts pipe in his mouth, and turns his profile to others.*]

TED. How about it?

MISS BROOKS. Very much in character.

COACH [*pleased*]. Just an idea I had.

MISS BROOKS [*eagerly*]. Oh, but it's a real help! An authentic touch.

TED [*considering it*]. I think I may get one of my own.

JANE [*meaning to be helpful*]. But wouldn't smoking cut down on your wind? [TED *scowls at her. She realizes her mistake and tries quickly to cover-up.*] It looks perfect, though. A pipe really suits you. [*Not pausing for breath.*] It makes you look like——

TED [*cutting in, not really taking himself so seriously*]. A big dope! [*Only half suppresses a chuckle, and* JANE *joins him in it. The shared chuckle embarrasses them, and they both withdraw a little.*] Anyway, it'll be fine for the play. [*Perches on one of desks near* JANE.]

JANE. Ideal.

COACH [*to* MISS BROOKS]. I came back to wish you good luck on the play and—everything.

MISS BROOKS. Thanks, Hugo.

COACH. I happened to pass the gym last night. You were working pretty late.

MISS BROOKS [*passing it off*]. Just clearing up odds and ends.

TED [*meaning to compliment her to* COACH]. Boy—she does all the work on the play—keeps classes going, marks papers, judges debates——

COACH [*meaning to be funny*]. And still has time to study up on sailing. [*It was the wrong thing to say.* MISS BROOKS *compresses her lips.*]

TED [*with smile, at* JANE]. At least she doesn't get you to hide basketballs, or personally makes off with the band instruments. [JANE *is also hurt and turns away. There is a pause.*]

MISS BROOKS [*to* JANE, *moving* L.]. We'd better assemble the cast. [JANE *nods and moves* L, *after her.*] The boys have quite a sense of humor.

TED [*jumping up*]. Hey, Jane——

COACH. Miss Brooks——

MISS BROOKS It's close to time. You gentlemen will have to excuse us. [*She and* JANE *go out* L.]

COACH. I must have said something.

TED. We both said something, only you especially. She didn't like that crack about studying up on sailing.

COACH. I was just trying to make a joke.

TED. Swell joke! All the work she does, and on top of it she studies up on sailing! To please you! And how do you show your appreciation? At a time the school board has her on the pan!

COACH [*stung*]. At least I don't gobble down three Swiss steaks and in the next breath suspect the person who gave them to me of embezzling the ticket money.

TED [*equally stung*]. I misunderstood.

COACH [*snapping*]. And your remarks about the basketballs and band instruments—they didn't help. [*Reprimanding.*] That's a darn sweet girl.

TED [*right back*]. I know it.

COACH. Then why don't you treat her better?

TED [*sitting on one of desks*]. Because I don't get a chance.

COACH. What's stopping you? [*Sits on desk near* TED.]

TED. Everything. [*After pause, no longer belligerent.*] I don't know how to handle it. You should see when she passes me in the hall.

COACH. Sort of distantly polite? [TED *nods.*] Same way with Miss Brooks.

TED. What bothers me is, after tonight, the play's over. [*Thinks about it.*] There's a place in the play where we're supposed to sort of—kiss. When we come to it tonight, I guess it'll sort of be—good-bye.

COACH. Maybe if you let her know how you feel——

TED. She's bound to know. I mean, when we get to that part in the play.

COACH [*thoughtfully*]. Too bad Miss Brooks and I——

TED. Miss Brooks and you—what?

COACH. Nothing. I was just thinking.

[*The door L opens and* MISS BROOKS *and* MARTIN *enter, followed by* JANE.]

MISS BROOKS [*to* MARTIN]. What is it you wanted to tell me? [*Pauses downstage of her desk with* MARTIN *and* JANE.]

MARTIN. This pain in my side. It's really sharp.

MISS BROOKS. Have you eaten anything special?

MARTIN [*shaking head*]. Perfectly normal diet. Cokes and potato chips.

MISS BROOKS [*a thought growing*]. Which side is it on?

MARTIN [*pressing his hand against his right side*]. Here.

COACH [*crossing to them*]. You don't suppose——

MISS BROOKS. What's it like?

MARTIN. Shooting pains. [*Pushes in with his hand.*] It feels hard.

TED [*concerned*]. Oh, oh!

MARTIN [*half laughing*]. Feels like what I really need is a big dose of salts.

MISS BROOKS. No, you don't!

MARTIN [*as a pain hits him*]. Golly!

MISS BROOKS [*to* JANE]. Call Miss Finch. [JANE *nods and goes out* R *quickly.* MISS BROOKS *speaks to* MARTIN.] You'll have to be looked at.

MARTIN [*moving to* C *stage, holding his side*]. Of all the dumb times to get a pain. [COACH *and* MISS BROOKS *move after* MARTIN.]

COACH. Maybe the hospital down the street . . . [MISS BROOKS *nods.*]

[JANE *enters* R *with* MISS FINCH.]

MISS FINCH. What is it? [*Comes to* C *with* JANE.]

MISS BROOKS [*to* MISS FINCH]. Do you have your car? [MISS FINCH *nods.*] There's a chance Martin has appendicitis.

MARTIN [*starting*]. What!

MISS FINCH. I'll run him right over.

MARTIN. Hey, wait a minute!

COACH [*seriously*]. You better go.

MARTIN. What about the play?

MISS BROOKS. What about Martin?

MISS FINCH. Come along. [*She and* MARTIN *go out* L. *Then* MISS FINCH *comes right back in.*] Say—what *about* the play? [MISS BROOKS *shrugs helplessly.* MISS FINCH *sighs and goes out* L *again.*]

COACH. What are you going to do?

TED. Everybody's out there—waiting.

[MARGE, ELSIE, *and* RHONDA *enter* L. *They come to* C.]

MISS BROOKS [*helplessly*]. What else could I do?

COACH. Darned if I know—but——

MARGE. Where's Martin going?

ELSIE. Anything wrong?

MISS BROOKS. He has a bad pain in his side.

MARGE [*nodding*]. He was complaining.

RHONDA. But where's he going?

COACH. Miss Finch is running him down to the hospital.

RHONDA. Just because he has a pain?

MARGE. Who's going to play the High Lama?

RHONDA [*dumbfounded*]. What about the play?
TED [*sharply*]. We're thinking about it.
RHONDA. What good does that do!
ELSIE. We *can't* stop the play now.
RHONDA [*to* MISS BROOKS]. I asked you—what are you going to do?
ELSIE. All the rehearsing and work, and everything——
RHONDA [*sharply*]. Miss Brooks!

[MR. WADSWORTH *and* MRS. ALLEN *enter* R.]

MR. WADSWORTH [*clapping his hands for action*]. Come—come——almost time! [*Moves to* R C *with* MRS. ALLEN.]
MRS. ALLEN. I'm so excited!
MR. WADSWORTH. Biggest turn-out we've ever had. [*To* MRS. ALLEN.] Do you want to tell her, or shall I?
MRS. ALLEN. You go ahead.
MR. WADSWORTH [*to* MISS BROOKS]. We've been discussing you. The school board held a meeting——
MISS BROOKS [*numbly*]. Discussing me?
MRS. ALLEN. Some of your unorthodox methods and procedures.
MR. WADSWORTH. And the 're not approved of, either. But the entire board seemed to feel the final result—what we mean is—the dress rehearsal was *magnificent*—finest play we've ever had! They all agreed—I'm directed to give you congratulations.
MISS BROOKS [*bewildered*]. Congratulations?
MRS. ALLEN [*delighted*]. You were splendid, Rhonda. We're all just overjoyed.
RHONDA [*near tears, hurrying to* MRS. ALLEN]. Mama—there isn't going to be any play. It's called off.
MRS. ALLEN. No play?
MR. WADSWORTH. Called off?
RHONDA. There won't be any play!
MR. WADSWORTH. Don't be silly.
MRS. ALLEN. What are you saying?
RHONDA [*ready to scream*]. I said—it's *all called off!*

MISS BROOKS [*weakly*]. Mr. Wadsworth . . .
MR. WADSWORTH [*his anger growing*]. What's she talking about?
MRS. ALLEN [*to* MISS BROOKS]. If you've spoiled that play—if you've spoiled it . . .
MISS BROOKS. You see——
COACH. One of the boys——
TED. Martin.
MARGE. He plays the High Lama.
MR. WADSWORTH [*trying to hold on to his sanity*]. What about him?
MISS BROOKS. I'm afraid he may be sick.
MR. WADSWORTH. You're *afraid*—he *may* be!
MISS BROOKS. There were signs of appendicitis——
MR. WADSWORTH. Where is he? What signs?
RHONDA. She sent him to the hospital!
MR. WADSWORTH. Sent him to the hospital? *Now?* [MISS BROOKS *nods dumbly.* MR. WADSWORTH *explodes.*] What about the play?
RHONDA. That's what I asked her.
MRS. ALLEN. Good heavens—it should be starting now.
MISS BROOKS. I was afraid—you see, if it *is* appendicitis——
MR. WADSWORTH. If it is appendicitis, of course—but how do you *know?*
MISS BROOKS. I just thought——
MR. WADSWORTH. Have you studied medicine?
MISS BROOKS. No, but——
MR. WADSWORTH. Have you *any* medical qualifications?
MISS BROOKS. No.
MR. WADSWORTH [*shouting*]. Then why'd you do it!
MISS BROOKS. I read an article once——
MR. WADSWORTH. Where?
MISS BROOKS. *Reader's Digest.*
MR. WADSWORTH. And on the basis of that?
MISS BROOKS [*decisively*]. Yes.

MRS. ALLEN [*decidedly, to* MR. WADSWORTH]. I think the board should re-convene Monday.

MR. WADSWORTH [*helplessly*]. What am I going to tell everyone? What am I going to do?

[MISS AUDUBON *enters* R.]

MISS AUDUBON [*brightly*]. The band's all ready. [*Pauses at* R *stage.*]

MR. WADSWORTH. Just hold it.

MISS AUDUBON. But it's time.

MR. WADSWORTH [*sharply*]. I said, hold it.

MISS AUDUBON. Yes, Mr. Wadsworth. [*Goes out* R.]

COACH [*to* MR. WADSWORTH]. The hospital's just down the street. Would you like me to see if they think Martin could go ahead?

MR. WADSWORTH. I'll phone myself.

MRS. ALLEN. Perhaps we could get him back, before it's too late.

MISS BROOKS [*helpfully*]. The band could play some extra numbers.

MR. WADSWORTH [*giving her a cold look*]. I'd better phone. [*Shakes his head with anger and warning.*] Brooks! [*Expels a breath and goes out* R.]

MRS. ALLEN [*following* MR. WADSWORTH *out* R, *pausing at door; bitterly, to* MISS BROOKS]. Some of our relatives have come hundreds of miles—just to see Rhonda.

MISS BROOKS. Maybe Martin has some relatives, too. [MRS. ALLEN *gives her a withering look and goes out* R. *There is a gloomy pause.*]

RHONDA. I think you did it on purpose. [*Goes out* L, *in tears.*]

MARGE. I better tell the others to relax. [*Hurries out* L.]

ELSIE. After the work we put in. [*Then smiles at* MISS BROOKS *ruefully.*] Gosh, I remember all my lines, now. [*Goes out* L.]

JANE. After the work *they* put in!

MISS BROOKS [*in commiseration, moving* D R, *sitting*]. They're so disappointed——

COACH [*moving toward her*]. But you did the right thing. [MISS BROOKS *gives him a look of appreciation.*] You did.

TED. Golly, Jane—I'm sorry.

JANE. Me, too.

TED. There was something I wanted you to know, and—well, at one place in the play—you'd know.

JANE. Ted—there's something I wanted *you* to know.

MISS BROOKS. I feel so awful.

COACH. If there was just something *I* could do. I used to be in plays. [*Shakes head.*] I couldn't learn a part that fast.

MISS BROOKS. It's an easy part, too. The High Lama doesn't move about. He stays in a chair upstage.

COACH. If the prompter could feed me the lines——

MISS BROOKS. Wouldn't work. [*Thoughtfully.*] He wears a big robe. Why couldn't you have a playbook open on your lap? No one could see.

COACH. And I could just read the lines—it wouldn't be good, but maybe it'd pass.

MISS BROOKS [*suppressing her excitement, rising*]. Hugo—would you? It might work!

COACH. Why not——Of course!

TED. My gosh!

JANE. The play could go on!

MISS BROOKS. Do you *know* the play at all?

COACH [*smiling*]. I read the book three times.

MISS BROOKS [*overjoyed*]. The playbooks—and Martin's costume—they're in my office.

COACH [*anxiously*]. I better look it over quick.

MISS BROOKS. Come on. [*Takes* COACH'S *arm and leads him out* U R C.]

JANE. Gosh!

TED [*relieved*]. I'm so glad!

JANE. We ought to tell Mr. Wadsworth—and Mrs. Allen.

TED. And Rhonda.

JANE [*taking a breath*]. Probably you'll be back with the sports car tomorrow.

TED [*nodding*]. My dad found a bargain. We're getting one of our own.
JANE [*delighted*]. You are? [*He nods.*] Could *I* come for a drive sometime?
TED. I want you to.
JANE. Ted. What you said—about what I'd know at a certain place in the play—is it—is it where I ask you, "Don't go"? [*He nods.*]
TED. And then you—[*She nods. He speaks with feeling.*]—and I wouldn't ever, you'll see.
JANE. Maybe you'll see, too—at the same place.
TED. I will?
JANE [*pulling away*]. We'd better call the others——
TED. Gosh, yes. [*He and* JANE *hurry out* L, *arm in arm.*]

[COACH, *with a robe over his arm and a playbook in his hand, enters* U R C. *He is followed by* MISS BROOKS.]

COACH [*coming to* C *with her*]. The way I remember—Conway has come to this Shangri-La—way off in the mountains. They've collected art and literature there, and the High Lama hopes it'll be safe from wars.
MISS BROOKS [*nodding*]. This leader at Shangri-La knows he's about to die—that's you—and you want Conway to carry on your work.
COACH. Here's his big speech.
MISS BROOKS. It's the heart of the play. Would you try it?
COACH [*reading—and reading well*]. "The storm outside will be such a one as the world has never seen before. There will be no safety in arms, no help for authority, no answer in science. It will rage till every flower of culture is trampled, and all human things are leveled in a vast chaos. I believe you will live through the storm. And after, through the long desolation, you will conserve the fragrance of history. You will welcome the stranger and teach him the rule of age and wisdom. Beyond that my vision weakens, but I see a new world stirring in the ruins, seeking its lost literature and legendary

treasures in that dark age. And they'll be here, preserved as by a miracle, for the new renaissance."

MISS BROOKS [*taking a breath*]. Thank you.

COACH [*quietly*]. Quite a play! [*After pause.*] It makes you wish there really was a Shangri-La.

MISS BROOKS [*hesitantly, thinking about it, moving and sitting at students' desk* L C.]. In a way a teacher makes her own Shangri-La. In a way she preserves these things by passing them on to her students. [*Laughs a little self-consciously*]. Though I don't think I'll ever get to the mountains of Tibet. [*Gives him a sideways look.*] Or even go sailing to Martinique and the Grenadines.

[MR. WADSWORTH *hurries in* R, MISS BROOKS *rises.*]

MR. WADSWORTH [*coming to* C]. Brooks—thank God you sent him right over. It *was* appendicitis!

MISS BROOKS. He's all right?

MR. WADSWORTH [*nodding*]. In plenty of time. I must have been out of my mind! [*Apologizes.*] I'm so terribly sorry for what I said.

[MISS AUDUBON *enters* R.]

MISS AUDUBON [*pausing by door*]. Should I start the band now?

MR. WADSWORTH. No.

MISS BROOKS. Yes! The play's going on. [*As* MR. WADSWORTH *turns in surprise.*] Hugo's going to handle the part.

MR. WADSWORTH. Hugo? [*To* COACH.] How can you?

COACH [*smiling*]. I've hidden talents.

MR. WADSWORTH. You do? [COACH *nods, smiling.* MR. WADSWORTH *turns to* MISS BROOKS.]

MISS BROOKS [*nodding*]. He does.

MR. WADSWORTH [*to* MISS AUDUBON]. Then get going.

MISS AUDUBON. Right away. [*Goes out* R, *followed by* MR. WADSWORTH.]

[ELSIE, RHONDA, MARGE, FAITH, JANE, TED, ELAINE, DORIS,

SYLVIA, *and* STANLEY *come in* L. *From off* R, *the school band strikes up an opening chord and plays as scene continues.*]

ELSIE. But how?
RHONDA. What about Martin?
MARGE. The Coach doesn't know the part.
FAITH [*to* JANE]. You're sure?
JANE. Positive!
TED. Get going. [*The members of* CAST *move to* C.]
ELAINE. I still don't see——
DORIS. Miss Brooks—is it true?
MISS BROOKS [*delightedly*]. *It's true!*
TED. See? [*Band starts playing off* R.]
MISS BROOKS. You hear. [*Checks her watch.*]
SYLVIA. That's it.
ELSIE. Oh, no! My lines!
MARGE. Don't think about them.
STANLEY. Coach—how come?
COACH. You handle your part—I'll handle mine.
MISS BROOKS. Take over, Sylvia. [SYLVIA *moves to door* R.]
TED [*taking* JANE'S *hand*]. Scared?
JANE. Not any more.
SYLVIA [*who has been checking her watch*]. Now—those in the first scene—take your places—Elaine, Faith, Stanley, Doris, Rhonda—on stage. [ELAINE, FAITH, STANLEY, DORIS, *and* RHONDA *go out* R.]
COACH [*to* MISS BROOKS]. About never sailing to Martinique and the Grenadines. We can discuss that later.
MISS BROOKS [*delightedly*]. Will we?
COACH [*nodding*]. Say, doesn't this part call for me to kiss **anybody**?
MISS BROOKS [*laughing*]. We can discuss that, too.
SYLVIA [*following her check sheet*]. Marge, Elsie—get ready—Ted—Jane . . . [MARGE *and* ELSIE *move to door* R.]
TED [*to* JANE, *at* R C]. Just a little while now, and—you'll know.
JANE [*sincerely*]. You'll know something, too. [*She and* TED

are holding each other's hand as they move to door R. *Curtain starts to fall.* ALL, *but* COACH *and* MISS BROOKS, *are looking anxiously out door* R.]

SYLVIA [*looking off* R *and calling to someone*]. Okay—raise it.

MISS BROOKS [*moving to door* R, *looking off.*] Curtain going up. [*Turns and starts toward* COACH.] This is the beginning. . . .

CURTAIN IS DOWN

WHAT PEOPLE ARE SAYING about *Our Miss Brooks*...

"This play has been a ball to do. My students have had fun and so have I. Also, it was such a wonderful insight into life in the '50s. Finally, the coach's speech at the end almost seems prophetic." *Drama Director,*
William T. Dwyer High School, Palm Beach Gardens, Fla.

"Timeless, easily adaptable to today, with themes that cross generations...love, friendships, and the stress of daily living at any age. *Our Miss Brooks* is a delightful journey to high school." *Teresa Fisher,*
Grundy Center High School, Grundy Center, Iowa

"It was so much fun to produce and the kids loved it. Great characters and a funny storyline." *Kirk Baldwin,*
Westmoreland High School, Westmoreland, N.Y.

"A rousing success. A wonderful comedy, the audience was in an uproar with laughter. A must-do comedy."
Art Roberson, North Love Christian School, Rockford, Ill.

"Highly entertaining. You would think it was written specifically for our school." *Jonathan Dyck,*
Landmark Collegiate, Landmark, MB Canada

"*Our Miss Brooks* was a rousing success. Our dessert theatre production brought in the most revenue ever, and people are still referring to the actors by their character names. The cast, audience and the director (me!) had a wonderful, memorable evening." *Claire Teague,*
Tacoma Baptist Schools, Tacoma, Wash.